Sex & Attention

Dedication

To everyone who has dealt with the biasness from the opposite sex. This book is dedicated to the freedom walkers and the freedom talkers who refused to be shackled by society's laws. And a special dedication to all the beautiful women who walked with me.

Especially my mother, I love you Linda. For all those nights you entered my room and I was sitting on the floor, by myself, doodling in my journal. Thank you mama, for all those days you came in and I was playing alone with my dollies. You never once judged me for being who I was. Even as a young child you knew I was different and you respected me. You were the first one to show me what it meant to truly be myself. You were the only one who ever came to all my performances. You believed in me and you knew your daughter was going to be a star, a creator. You did what a great parent would, you trusted me. You allowed me to use my free will and never once made me feel ashamed for it.

You are my angel.

Books by Sasha Owens

Voices Unveiled

Sex & Attention

Sex & Attention

Contents

Prologue

One thing I am not... is a bad person. I've sat in my room many nights questioning my actions and replaying the sentences spoken about me. As a woman, we are expected to act a certain way and we aren't allowed to do those things that men do because see... that makes us a hoe. Why is a woman who is in charge of her sexuality considered a hoe? If a guy has a ménage à trois, a foursome, or bangs a group of friends then he's the man. However, if a woman should do those things she is automatically the scum of the earth. A harlot, a whore, a slut, a hoe, a bitch. A woman is called just about any name you can think of that is degrading, double standards. If a woman wants to have a ménage à trois, men will find a way to degrade that and say she had a "train ran on her." But that statement is neither here nor there. This is a story of a woman who loves sex. She loves everything about it, but she isn't a whore. Oh no, she chooses her players very precisely and they choose her back. There are no rules to who your pussy clenches to when they look in your eyes. It is true, a woman knows the moment she meets a guy if she will have sex with him. What most women do is we bury the feeling deep into our minds until something happens that won't make us seem whorish. There are moments when we want to play those games and there are moments when we can't. There is an electrifying pull stronger than gravity between two people who have sexual tension, but are trying to suppress it. Men have it so easy they don't have to suppress it.

Well, if you have ever thought any of these things or if you're just intrigued, then you are in the right place. I want to take you on a ride with me along with two lovers I had. They both rocked my world. They both changed me. They awakened me. I met them in different ways.

For one I prayed and for one preyed me.

Chapter 1
<u>Meeting</u>

I rolled out of bed that morning and went straight to the bathroom to brush my teeth. I cannot stand morning breath it's totally disgusting. I was somewhat exhausted from another night of hearing my roommate have wild, crazy sex, and here I was still on the celibacy train. I honestly should've gotten off of it a long time ago. I was abstaining from sex in hopes of being blessed with a husband and giving myself to him. Hilariously, the man I had loved all my life dumped me and married some chick with three kids and no high school diploma. What a way to knock a girl's self-esteem down. I always thought I was good enough and surely a woman who is waiting for the Lord to send her husband will get one. I guess it just doesn't work that way. I should have probably been happy that she saved me from a heartache of pain because marriage didn't stop him from cheating. But nevertheless, here I was staring at my dimples in the mirror, my long "Poetic Justice" braids, brown skin, and full breast as my toothbrush thrust in and out of my mouth. I spit in the sink and grabbed my mouthwash. It was something about the mint flavor that I loved.

My heart had been convicted and honored to saving my body for a special man for nearly three years, but I made my mind up that when I met a guy that this year I was choosing to break it. I no longer wanted to wait. I wanted to feel anything.

My roommate then burst into my bathroom.

"Vistoria, I hope you're ready for the meeting today," said Kara.

Kara's name is actually Takara, but no one ever calls her that. The other letters just aren't needed.

Kara was in some network-marketing thing and wanted me to give it a try. I had agreed to go to the informational meeting with her just to see what all the fuss was about. I had been seeing the name all over my Instagram timeline, Live Lavish. Which was definitely the opposite of what I was doing. I walked out of the bathroom and went into my room to grab something to wear. I picked this black dress because it was the most simple. I threw it over my head and watched as it hugged all my curves. I was a tad bit insecure of how much it accentuated my figure. All through my celibacy I relinquished all my sexy clothing as to not arouse men in any way. The dress had a V-cut which hugged my Double D's and my stomach was cinched to the gods after all the fasting I had been doing while I waited for my husband. My butt, well it wasn't very big, but the dress hugged it nice as well. The dress was a good accent next to my caramel skin. I walked down the hallway to see if my roommate had gotten dressed. She had on a cute one-piece body suit that hugged her curves. Her natural curly hair was in one giant puffball.

"You look nice," I said. She turned around.

"Oh my gosh, but not as nice as you. I haven't seen those things in years," she said as she honked my boobs like horns.

We arrived at the meeting early and Kara's mentor had us setting up in preparation for the others to arrive. I took a seat in the audience as

Kara prepared some things around the podium. Business partners and prospects began to flood the room and I observed them all. After hearing the key speakers I decided that I would join also.

"So I'm ready to sign up," I said to Kara.

She showed me the link to her profile at livelavish.com/weonlycarryhundreds.

"Really? 'We only carry hundreds' is your business page?" I asked.

"Yea, I'm trying to make sure I appeal to all the drug dealers with money too."

"Shoot anyone can do this business because it's not a background check, all you need is your $100 membership fee and Internet access."

This was going to be my first network marketing company, but I could tell I was going to enjoy it because of the travel package. I loved to travel and they had so many exclusive deals. There was a deal to the Bahamas for $189 for 5 days and 4 nights.

That's insane and you cannot beat those prices.

I felt like I was getting the best of both worlds. I was making money and saving money. I had so many mentors in the company who had switched from making $600 a month to $6,000, $10,000, all the way up to $140,000 monthly. That was exactly the break I needed because I hadn't been working for a while. After graduation I took a break from everything. Life, people, jobs, but now it was time to get back into the swing of things. I didn't necessarily want to get a 9-5 so this was great because I was my own boss and I could focus on my acting and writing career as well. In that season I learned one of the greatest luxuries you could have is your time because you can choose when to get up, how much money you make that day, and when you stop working. It was an amazing thing. I was taking calls and jotting things down for my new book all at the same time. I also liked the support I got from my mentors and my uplines. We all were in a group chat where we went when we added new people, needed to ask questions, or if we just needed to discuss the business. It was good to keep all the matters between people who were in the company and not to be out discussing it all over social media. That was bad for business.

I stayed up most of my first night after I joined just writing notes and listening to videos that discussed how successful people had made this work for them. I decided that once I became familiar with the training videos I would start sharing the business with people on my social media. After that I would follow up with a call to my upline for further questioning.

I was successful in this business very fast. I easily became a top earner in the company. It was so exciting adding all my people to the group chat when I had gotten new team members. I loved getting the praise from my colleagues. I was proud that I was making it work. Two a day, Three a day, Four a day. It was increasing and increasing. I was getting all the attention until one day I wasn't. Another team member started to add people just as fast as me. I clicked on the name to see whom this was competing with me. It was some guy named Varus. I wasn't mad about it, but I was very curious. I was the shining new star and someone was leveling the plain. I was always happy when other people had members join; it was all good for the company. It was interesting to see someone getting people as fast as I was. Everyone kept saying congrats as he added more and more people to the chat. It appeared that a lot of people knew him before the company. The chat always went wild when he added someone.

Lavish Chat 1

Britt: Congrats Zay.

Shana: Good job Zay.

Bruce: I see ya Zay. Apply pressure.

Varus: 'Preciate it.

I clicked on his icon and it took me to his Hangout page. Varus Phillips. I was a tad bit confused because I didn't know if it was the same person. I looked again and he was the one who was replying back. I guess Zay was just his nickname. His picture was kind of small and I couldn't see much, but he didn't look that cute.

Typical ugly guy syndrome. He has the hard worker gene because he can't pull chicks any other way.

I laughed.

It was late that night and we all were in the chat just having fun and sharing our success stories from earlier in the day. We all decided to be more personable and finally add each other on social media. I added Zay pretty fast because I was waiting to see how his social media was and then I got the shocker of a lifetime. He was attractive. I mean this man was fine. The little picture in the chat had done him no justice at all. I was all over his page. His cousin Lennox had dropped his social media too. Kara and I were being thirst buckets trying to decide which one we should go after. Lennox was so fine, but it was something about Zay that attracted me more. It was something about him that I wanted to get to know. Zay also seemed to be a little rougher around the edges, which was my type of guy. I chose to close in on Zay, it had been a while since I had been with any guy but it was something about him. Something about him made me want to give up my three years of being celibate. I was tired. My love life had failed. I had waited. My patience was gone. I wanted him. Simple. I didn't really care how it happened, but I had spotted my target.

A few days later I got in the chat and saw that he had hit a new level in our company. It was called Star 3 and it's when you start earning a good residual amount with the company. I decided to congratulate him outside of the group chat. I wrote him on Facebook.

Varus Xavier Phillips

Congratulations on
Star 3 Zay.

Thanks, I'm trying
to get like you.

Oh whatever, you're
already better than me.

9

You've been adding
people every day and
I've slowed down
some.

You the one with
all the money.
And I feel like
I could be doing
more.

Well, I think you're
doing an awesome
job. You just started
and you're already
at Star 3. That's
faster than I made
it.

Well I need some
help getting
to the next
level. Do you
think you could
give me some
pointers?

Sure, just text me.
(143) 690-8976.

I was so excited that we had exchanged
numbers. He was so sexy. That 6'2, caramel skin,
with tattoos placed on the most beautiful muscle
physique. Art. I sat there wondering.

10

Does he really just want business tips or is he into me?

You wouldn't believe how insecure I had gotten when it came to super attractive men. Being celibate that long had made me slightly awkward and less confident around them.

If we have sex would I even be any good? It has been so long. I may just suck and I'm not talking about orally.

So he finally text me and you wouldn't believe what we talked about. We talked about the business for hours. It really seemed as if he was intrigued because I had so much knowledge. I wasn't going to be a little thot-whore and deter the conversation so I answered the questions. Although it wasn't exactly where I was hoping the conversation would go I enjoyed texting him. I even did a few 3-way calls for him when our other uplines were too busy to do a closing call. He said he liked how I conversed with the prospects and really gave them the information. We got really close over that period of time with handling business.

I knew I had to find a way to get him out of the phone world and in my actual presence, but I didn't know how. The Universe must've heard my cry because one of our uplines from Texas had decided to fly in for the weekend and he wanted to meet with his Star 3 and higher team in Memphis, TN. This made my day because I knew I was going to finally get to meet Zay in person.

OMG I have to look awesome. I gotta find something professional and sexy.

Our upline, Lennox text us when he had gotten in town that day. He was trying to decide if he should get a rental or see if me or Kara could pick him up. Kara and I always had things to do, like the mall and to get our nails done so we told him he would probably want to get a rental. It wasn't that we had a problem picking him up we just knew we could be all day in this mall trying to find the perfect thing to wear. Oh yea, I neglected to mention that Kara had a long-time crush on Lennox. They had a moment in college together that never really went anywhere. Lennox tried to deny it like he didn't have any prior memories of her before the company, but we both knew that was a lie. We let him continue to believe it though.

We let the guys choose a place to eat at. They chose Chili's, which I was happy with because I loved Chili's. It was either that or a bar, but Lennox claimed he didn't want to make me feel uncomfortable. My strict religious life was kinda well known to most people, but what they didn't know was that I was slowly ready to break free from that. I hadn't done anything other than breath and attend church for the last three years. However, I respected the sincerity of the act.

Kara and I got dressed in the same room. We did this often so we could analyze our clothing and makeup. I had on this cute top with a skater skirt. My top of course was cut in the boob area. My boobs were nice so I loved showing them off. I had my hair in long individual braids that were near my butt. I decided to wear them up in a cute bun that night. Kara but on a cute pink top and some high-waisted jeans that really made her butt look nice. We left our apartment and drove ten minutes up the road to the restaurant. We both were kinda nervous because this was more than just a business meeting. There was plenty of crushing to go around. We walked up to the entrance of the door and they were already standing there. Lennox was dressed in between street nigga and businessman while shining bright like the light above their head at the restaurant entrance. His fade was just right with his curly hair low. And then there was Zay. Zay was gorgeous. He was even more delectable in person. I hugged Lennox first so my attraction to Zay wouldn't seem as obvious. However, when I did finally hug him I was melting in his arms. He smelled so good and that 6' 2" body just looked like a tree I wanted to climb, over and over again.

We got seated at our table and the jokes began. We talked a little about the business but it was mostly just getting personable with each other. Lennox kept pointing out that I was the only one not drinking at the table.

"Why don't you drink?" Zay asked me.

"I'm just not much of a drinker so one drink will already have me buzzed and I'm driving," I replied.

"So what are y'all doing after this?" Lennox asked.

"Probably just going back to the house while being bored out of our minds," Kara said.

That was Kara's way of letting it be known I'd rather be doing something else with you. I was hoping he picked it up and suggested something else to do because I surely wasn't finished looking at Zay yet. So we talked it over and they decided they wanted to go to this popular club to enjoy the rest of the night.

"So you coming or nah?" Zay asked me.

"Well it appears Kara wants to go now and I am the driver so I don't have much of a choice."

In clubs in Memphis you can skip to the front of the lines if you know somebody on the inside, like the owner or the bouncer. You can also just pay to get in the VIP line, which moves faster than the regular line. We all just paid the extra; it is not cool standing in a long line with heels on. Once we got in the club Zay and Lennox headed straight for the bar area.

Lennox asked, "So you drinking here? Or you still gone be lame?"

"Gimme a shot of Goose," I said.

Grey Goose was my signature drink when I was trying to get a buzz and enjoy myself quick. One shot would get me going, two and I would be really good, three or more and you were about to see the other Vistoria come out.

"Stori, how many have you taken so far?" asked Kara.

"I have no idea, I lost count a long time ago," I replied. I whispered in her ear, "Zay is so sexy, I want to do him like now."

I moved in closer to him and started a conversation. The club began getting super packed and the walk way was now filled with people, which made it hard for traffic to move freely. I tried to get as close to the bar as I could so people could get by and then I thought of a plan. The next time someone got too close to me I was going to back up on Zay and make sure I got closer each time. Someone walked by and I backed up right on his package.

"Oops, I'm sorry, it's so crowded in here I'm running out of places to move," I said.

"Naw, you good," he replied.

That was my entrance I was going to test this thing out and see how his body language reacted to me being on him. Each time I got closer and closer to the point where now the club was so crowded that my butt was permanently against his package.

I looked up to him, "If you want me to get off you just say it," I laughed.

He placed his hands around my waist and pulled me in more. It was then that it was confirmed. He wanted me too.

Lennox was over there trying to close in on Kara and then it happened...

Cash Money Records taking over for the 99 and the 2000's

Next thing I know Kara and I lost it all over them. This song is religious in the club. If you can dance, then you dance. If you can't, then you better pretend. If you're southern you don't try to act classy off this song. Class leaves the building and your trap queen and enter ratchet goddess must come forth.

It is moments like this that I'd like to demonstrate exactly what Clatchet truly is. I remember making sure my circles were just right, grazing his pelvic area, oh-so perfectly. I also did my signature move of bouncing on him. I made sure my feet were firmly on the ground, I grabbed his pants with my hands and as I threw it back, I would pull him into me. It's basically my way of mimicking doggy-style standing up. I needed Zay to get this hint without me having to say it. After that I bent over and touched my toes and worked him that way until the song went off. Oh yea, another rule in southern club etiquette is you dance until the song goes off. I don't care if your stomach muscles are getting tired, you keep dancing. Small circles will suffice but you don't stop moving. This is bible. So as the song ended I stood back up and placed my head in the cusp of his neck and shoulder.

Then he said to me, "I can't lie Stori, I want you right now."

I turned around and now we were facing each other and whispered back in his ears, "I'm all yours, just tell me how you want me."

Where did that come from? I guess my inner freak is deciding to come out to play tonight.

I scurried through the aisles of the grocery store in need of my go-to sobering meal. I normally grabbed a turkey sandwich and packed it with all the veggies I could think of and guggle down an orange juice. However, tonight I didn't feel like carrying a loaf of bread around, so I was going to need a backup plan.

Light Bulb!

I decided that a Lunchable would do the trick. I grabbed two turkey and cheese lunchables

16

just in case one didn't do it. This was a trick I learned in college from my many 5'o clock nights and 8'o clock morning classes. College is the time where you either crack under the party life pressure or you make it your bitch. I was never one to crack under anything. I would convince myself that being intoxicated was a mental thing, piss, and eat something bread-based. I must say this exact thing helped me in classes and helped me one time I got stopped by an officer. Well it was either that I convinced him or my boobs got me off. Nonetheless, I was grateful.

Oh, yeah back to the story at hand.

When I got back in the car I text Zay and asked for his address.

"Girl what are we waiting on? I'm ready to have Lennox's cock in me," Kara said.

"I just text Zay and asked him for the address but he hasn't responded yet," I said.

"Oh girl, I'm two steps ahead of you. I got the address from Lennox while you were in the store," she replied.

"Oh cool, text it to me so I can just do the GPS from my phone," I said.

Luckily, his apartment was close to the club so I didn't have to use all my brainpower I had left to focus on driving for a long time. When I was almost there I got a text message from Zay with the address. It was late but at least I knew for sure he still wanted me to come.

How embarrassing would that be to show up and he's asleep or even worse he's just loss interest or invited another chick over?

The thought was piercing, but I was happy it wasn't the case.

Kara and I drove around the complex trying to find the right apartment. This was always confusing looking for building numbers in the dark. It's even worse when you're slightly buzzed and trying to find it. My Grey Goose had worn off a lot by now. I called Zay when I finally made it to the right building because I still didn't know what apartment number it was.

"Oh, over there. I see him," Kara said.

Zay came to stand outside with his shirt off. I was beginning to melt inside from the thought that I was moments away from lying down with him.

As I walked in I noticed there were boxes everywhere. Lennox came from one of the rooms near the back and pulled Kara back there with him. I followed Zay back to his room. He had some soft R&B music playing. I looked around the room and it smelt of some kind of incense. From what I could see from the glistening of the moon peering in from the blinds it was really neat in here. It just had that vibe of someone who was clean. I knew he worked out, but it didn't wreak of sweaty gym shorts or dirty sneakers. I had taken my shoes off by now and the carpet was nice and soft under my feet.

"So what's with all the boxes? Are you moving in or moving out?" I asked.

"I'm moving into a house not too far from here," he said.

"I'll be needing that address as well," I

smiled.

"Come here, why you way over there?" he reached for me.

I moved in closer to him and he slowly lifted my head and started to kiss me on my neck. I moved my head around to catch his bottom lip. I began sucking on his lip and he slid his tongue into my mouth. I started to suck on his tongue and he worked his fingers into my panties. I could feel my juices start to flow out of me and surround his fingers. His hands were now able to move freely as my wetness worked as a lubricant. He laid me down on the bed and pulled my skirt off and then my underwear. He grabbed a condom from the dresser on side of the bed and he slowly entered me. I felt my body welcoming him. I began to gush out even more as he stroked. I was shocked I was handling this so well being that it had been three years since my last partner. My guess is it was the liquor relaxing me because I'm sure my sober mind would've been tensing and making this painful. I started to grind up as he stroked. He moved in circles and not just an in and out movement. I remember thinking that with each circle he was hitting every inch of me. He came in that position and I came right along with him. He rested on my chest for a moment after he came and then rolled over to the side of me.

"So I guess Zay comes from Xavier, if I'm right?" I asked.

"Yes," he replied.

"Why do people always pull Zay out of Xavier? Why not just X or Vier?" I asked jokingly.

"It's probably for the same reason people pull Dick from Richard or Bob from Robert. It's just something familiar that stuck. If it's not broke then why fix it?" he stated as if we were in court and he had to plead his case.

"Ok, ok I get it," I said. "I'll let up on your nickname," I laughed.

I got up to use the restroom and I looked at myself in the mirror. It was a good thing I had braids that way I didn't end up with, "I've just been fucked hair." I admired my tight, yet thick physique I had acquired from my recent eating habits and working out.

When I came out of the bathroom I went and laid next to Zay, but I didn't get too close to him. I knew certain men liked their space. However, it wasn't too long before he moved in next to me and cuddled me.

"Make sure you come home tomorrow," he whispered.

I looked at him to see if he was awake or sleep talking.

What does he mean by home?

I just sat there quiet because I didn't really know how to reply to that comment.

"I have to go to work in the morning, but you can stay here until I get off. You don't have to leave," he mumbled.

He sounded like he was bargaining with me, as if he really wanted me to be here when he got off work.

"Maybe we can do something once I get back," he continued.

20

"Ok," I finally fixed my mouth to say something.

It was hard to tell if this was just sleep talking, so I didn't get my hopes up to possibly think he was that much into me.

I mean I did just kinda have sex on the first night. Which isn't something I think is so horrible but gosh men sure do. I don't think they care while they're in the moment, but later this is the demonstration on why a woman can't be trusted. Which is a false representation. Clearly there's some girl in the world making one guy wait for 90 days and she busts it wide open for another one in the same night of meeting him. There really are no rules or one way to look at these things. I believe the best solution is for people to get to know whomever you're dealing with personally and not judge by such petty things as how soon someone had sex with you. Honestly, in moments like now if the energy is there I say I am denying myself to fight off all this pressure that was building up.

My rapid thoughts were interrupted by Zay's snoring. I had an entire conversation to myself about what I had just done. I decided it was time for me to get some sleep too so I inhaled his smell one more time. Something about him just gave me a peace.

I woke up early the next morning and Zay was still sleeping. I looked at him and I wanted to stay with him. But what I figured we were and what had happened last night stopped me. I convinced myself there was no need to stay in bed with him and pretend we were anything more than

sex partners, cuddy buddies, or a one-night stand. I
guess whichever name for it floats your boat. It
was darn good so I totally didn't resent having
another moment with him, but I knew I couldn't
get my feelings involved. I slid my underwear
back on, then my skirt. I latched my bra back and
put on my shirt. I slid on my shoes and grabbed
my purse. I kissed him softly and I headed for the
hallway. I knocked lightly on the door of the room
I had saw Lennox come from earlier. No one
came. I text Kara's phone.

Kara Poo <3

Are you ready to go?
Or are you getting a ride
back to the house
from Lennox?

I just opened my eyes.
Let me put my clothes
back on.

Whore! Lol ok.

I have so much to tell you.

I stood by the front door and waited for
Kara to come out. She entered the hallway and
because she didn't have braids she definitely had,
"I've just been fucked hair." I locked the door from
the inside and pulled the door up.

Kara and I got home and went our separate
ways. I went straight to my bathroom and took a
shower. I had a few light hickeys on me. I smiled.
I let all my clothing drop on the floor one by one
and I slid into the shower. The heat from the
shower felt so good against my skin. Our air

conditioner had been running while we were gone, so it was freezing in our house. I grabbed my towel and I lathered it with my soap. I cleaned all my body and then I picked up my loofah. I added my favorite lavender body wash to it. I loved to do this last and let all the suds roll over my body. I washed all the suds off of my body, turned the water off, and stepped out of the shower. I lifted one foot and dried it and then I lifted the other. Once I was dry I stepped out onto the pretty, pink rug in my bathroom. I hung the towel on the rack and walked to my bed and I just fell on it. I just wanted to lie there for a moment and reflect on my night.

I started to drift off then I heard a knock on the door.

"Stori, Stori, you up?"

It was Kara.

"Yea, barely. Come in," I replied.

She ran and jumped in my bed.

"Do you ever wear clothes?" I asked.

"No, and especially not at home," she laughed.

"Who needs clothes anyways? I sure don't," she kissed me on my cheek. "We soooo have to catch up on our nights."

She looked at me with stars in her eyes.

"I need ALL the details. Like I need to know if it was good. I need to know if it was bad."

I took her through the story.

"OMG he told you to come home? What does that mean anyways? He's like totally into you," she smirked and nodded her head.

"I don't know about all that. He was super drunk. Did you see all the drinks he had? I do believe it was simply just the liquor talking. For all I know he could have very well been confusing me with someone else he's talking to. I mean he did have all those boxes and he said he was moving. Maybe he's moving in with some chick," I pessimistically stated.

"Stori. 1st off, breath when you talk. Gosh you ramble on and on. 2Nd stop assuming. You're like the Queen of that," Kara teased.

"I may be the Queen, but then you would surely be the Princess. You're clearly assuming he likes me more than he's said," I snarked back.

"Ok, I'll let you have that one," she said. "Even though he also asked you to stay and hang out when he got off work. You're the one who left and didn't even wait for him to wake up," she defended.   "Because I know how these things go and I'm fine with that. I don't have to be with him in a serious manner. It was just good sex and after the heartbreak I've had recently, that's good enough for me. Love may never feel the same for me," I exhaled.

The room was quiet for a moment.

"Well I've given you all the juice on my night. Spill it," I said excitedly.

"For starters, I need to go to Wal-Mart and get a Plan B," she covered her face.

"What?!" I exclaimed. "You guys had unprotected sex already? Crazy little freaky things," I joked.

"Oh shut up, we did use a condom but it

24

broke. Then when it broke, he just kept going," she said.

"So there's potentially a little Lennox inside of you?" I asked.

"Yes, and he keeps texting me asking if I've went and got it yet," she laughs.

"You know how those trust fund babies can be. He's making sure nothing pulls any of his income," I rolled my eyes.

"He's a mess, girl don't nobody want his lil' money," she replied.

"It's always hilarious to me how men get themselves in this situation and then it's our job to get them out. We are either stuck getting the Plan B pill, the abortion, or taking care of the kid. Like seriously, when are they going to step up and take responsibility? But I guess that's another argument for another day," I said irritably.

"Uh oh, Stori. Your feminist side is showing," she teased.

"Oh please, spare me!" I said and grabbed my chest.

We both started laughing. We finished exchanging all the details about our night during the drive to Wal-Mart for Kara's Plan B pill. When we arrived back home I went and got back in bed and put my face under the covers. I was very much addicted to being in my bed. That was one of the perks I had found in network marketing. I could pretty much be anywhere and share the business with someone. Being an aspiring writer this gave me more time to work on projects and to meet deadlines. I went to sleep and woke up with my phone vibrating and tons of messages. Most of them were from the group chat with our team. I opened the message from Kara first.

Kara Poo <3

Get in the chat.
Hello.
Are you sleep?
Or are you in there masturbating?

I just woke up lol.
I'm going in now.

Lavish Chat 1

Lennox: Y'all sleep ain't it? Who really out here working?

The nerve of him to be in this chat asking who out here working. He should be working his ass to the drugstore to get that Plan B pill instead of having Kara go as if she nutted in herself.

I liked Lennox but no one was exempt when it came to doing shiesty things to my friends.

Varus: I'm about to go pass some flyers out now.

Lennox: Where my Memphis, TN team? All y'all need to be going out with Zay to pass out fliers for our next event.

Cruise: I can make it.

We had a big event coming up where a lot of our top earners were flying in and we needed to get as many prospects to the event as possible. They were flying out on their own tab and it was up to us to make it worth their while. We really needed to have the majority of our prospects all sign up. The meeting was going to be at the closing of the next month, which was perfect. It was always good to finish the month strong.

Lavish Chat 1

Kara: I'll go out.

Vistoria: I'm all in. Let's get it.

Timothy: That's what I like to hear ladies. Y'all stepping up to the plate.

Lennox: Well I flew out this morning so I can't make it, but I'll see y'all at the next event. Hit me up if y'all need something.

I figured this would give me another chance to have an excuse for meeting up with Zay. I liked using business as a way to get my pleasure. I didn't want to seem all clingy or like I was crowding him, so this worked out well for me. I decided to text him to see what time he was going to head to pass out fliers.

Zay

Hey! What time are your peeps going to pass fliers out?

I get off work today around 3, so somewhere around that time. Where y'all going to pass them out at? We should all link up.

Yea, that's what I was

thinking too. It's always good when people can see the team. That way they know they're not alone.

Ok, cool. So I'll see y'all then.

Ok, see you soon. I'm going to go print some of the fliers out at Office Depot.

Yea, I'm about to print some here at my job.

Cool, well I'll text you when we get to the mall.

I decided to hit Kara up to make sure she was still going.

Kara Poo <3

Hey are you still going to meet up to hang some fliers?

Girl, I wanted to, but this Plan B done made my period come on. This is my 1st time using it I didn't know that would happen.

I take it you didn't read the side effects

sheet? I suppose a
period is better
than being pregnant
in your case.

Oh whatever, I think
I might can push
through and pass
a few out in our
neighborhood.
Did you wanna go
now or later?

That's fine. We can
go pass some out
now.

Kara and I walked the neighborhood and
went in a few stores near where we lived and
posted fliers for the event and talked to people who
already had an interest. We got a lot of people who
said they were going to come out. It was nearing
the time for me to meet Zay and the others at the
mall so we headed back towards our house. I got in
my car and drove up the street. The mall was close
to where I lived in Midtown. When I got there I
sent a text to Zay letting him know I had arrived.
He informed me he was there and we met by the
entrance.

"So where's everybody at?" I asked.

"I've been texting them, but it seem like
they running late or aint gone make it," he replied.

"Well I guess we can go ahead and get
started and just count the mall as one of the places
we went. They can either catch up or just go pass

29

them out somewhere else," I said.

I made sure I was keeping it professional and not taking this as a moment to act like we were together. I kept a great distance between us as we were walking. I walked in a few stores alone and met back up with him. We met at the sitting area in the mall and talked to a few people over there. Zay moved closer to me and began rubbing on my hands.

Public affection?

I blushed and smiled back at him, but I was very confused. I didn't get why he was breaking the rules that were supposed to be at play here. We decided to make one more trip around the mall. We had come in on the top floor so now it was time to do the bottom and just see if we could connect with some people. I had posted on social media that we were there sharing the business so I had some prospects who came up. I spoke with them and Zay helped out. It was nice working together and for a moment I felt something. I felt like we could do some great things together. There were many successful people in this company and I just thought of how we had helped each other get ahead thus far. How great it would be if we were like a power couple of the company. I didn't entertain the thought very long because everything with us was still very new. We were walking back through the mall headed to our cars and he put his hands in between mine. It felt so right but then it was terrifying. I knew I could fall in love with him, but I didn't know if that's what these things meant.

It's sad that men these days do all these things that make a woman feel special and make her feel there's something more between them. This is only until she takes what they do seriously and believes that it means he wants her in a deeper way. It's like the moment a woman breaks her guard and allows a man in that's the same moment that the man takes the exit. He starts to act funny, he starts to text less. So it was because of this reason I just didn't want to believe that any of these gestures of public affection meant anything more than maybe he wanted to have sex again tonight. He didn't have to put in so much work for it though. I wish men would realize that too. There are times when a woman just wants sex too and all the extraness is just delaying the process. Get to the point. We don't want to waste time. I actually respect the honesty. I'd rather you tell me straight up that you're interested in sex only so I can weigh that option than for you to tell me you're interested in more and I get my heart involved only to find out you were lying because you thought it was the only way to get you sex. Oh, it is a nasty, never ending cycle. But the moral of the story is to keep it real because only real is respected.

By the time I zoned back in Zay had walked me to my car. I stood by the door for a moment and just looked up at him. He leaned in and he kissed me on my forehead.

"Have you eaten anything? You wanna go grab a bite to eat before you head home?" he asked.

"Sure," I haven't eaten since earlier.

31

We stopped by this popular Cajun restaurant because they served his favorite thing, fish. I had the pasta and it was delicious. He gave me this look as if I was something special to him. I would look up after I had taken a bite and he was gazing at me with a smile. I felt special when I was with him. And just like that it was already starting to happen. I knew I was going to have to start the fight to protect my heart because it was starting to seem as if he was after me.

After our meal we went back to my place because it was closer. Before we could even make it in the house good he was all over me. He kissed me and I leaned back against the wall. His kisses seemed to carry me off my feet. He spun me around into another wall. I didn't know if Kara was there or not but at the moment I didn't care. His passion was liberating me. We finally made it to my room and I remember my body hitting the bed and floating like a feather. I felt so at peace with him. He was gentle yet aggressive with me and it was a perfect blend. He was easily my most favorite sex partner out of all my years. He came while I was in the doggy-style position. I was starting to get more comfortable with the size of his penis in me. I allowed him to pull my waist into his pelvic area as rough and deep as he liked. This position filled my stomach all the way up with his cock, but I enjoyed it because he enjoyed it so much. I did like that I got my moments to throw it back in positions like this. I couldn't do it while he was digging deeper, but the moments where he got tired I could fill in with a few circles and bounces. I would move on him just like I did that night at the club, but the only difference is he was inside of me now.

Chapter 2
<u>Inside</u>

A few weeks had gone by and it seemed as if I had spent every moment with Zay. We were really getting close and I enjoyed it. He made me laugh and he challenged me. We helped each other to excel in many ways.

Zay

What you doing Lil' Stori?

> I've yet to figure out why I have to get Lil' at the front of my name lol. But I'm just over here working on a writing project.

You should come over.

> What time are you getting out of church?

I didn't go today.

> Can I work if I come over there? I really gotta knock this out for a contest I'm entering.

Sure, come on.

So I put my laptop in its case and packed all the things I would need while I was over there. I took a few snacks as well because Zay only had protein bars and muscle milk. I used those

35

sometimes but not as much as he did. I hopped in the shower just to freshen up. I never knew if I was going to be greeted with his penis or actually just chilling. I went to my closet and stared for a while trying to decide what I should put on. I decided to put on something cute but comfy. I chose a crop top and some leggings. My butt looked nice in these and of course my boobs were awesome in the crop top. I put my braids up in a bun and did some eyebrows with a little eye shadow. I didn't feel a need to put on a full face of makeup. Thankfully, from eating pretty healthy and drinking plenty of water my skin was normally clear as long as I wasn't PMSing.

His new house was a 20-minute drive from me. I turned on some pop music and jumped all over my car the ride there. I liked listening to music that kept my spirits high and mad me happy. I was pulling into his driveway before I knew it. I noticed that it was some other cars there too. He had some other friends who lived there with him and it seemed like they always had someone over. I got out the car and walked to the door and knocked lightly. I could hear them listening to some game.

Men.

One of his friends opened the door and gave me a frisky look. I walked in and spoke to everyone and headed to Zay's room. I sat down on the bed and pulled my laptop out. Zay walked in with laundry so I knew where he had just come from.

"If I had known it was laundry day I

would've brought mine over too," I teased him.

"I mean you could have, you just was gone be doing it yourself," he replied.

"Uh, that's defeating the purpose. I want you to do it," I joked back.

I continued typing on my laptop as he did his house chores. He sat down for a moment near me and watched TV for a moment. I guess he had to catch up with the game. He then got back up. Before he walked away he leaned over and kissed me on my forehead.

"Where are you off to now?" I asked.

"About to go lift weights for a lil' bit," he said.

"Ok, well don't be gone too long," I smiled.

I worked a little more on my laptop and then I put it back in the case. My brain was getting tired and I had been juggling a few marketing calls as well. He came back in after his workout and headed for the bathroom. I heard the shower start.

In moments he was climbing into bed with me. He put his arm around me and pulled me close. I listened to his breathing.

"How do you feel if I decided to go back to being celibate?" I asked.

"I mean, it's ultimately your choice. I'd miss being intimate with you, but I wouldn't try to stop you," he said.

"Would I still be invited over? Or would that be the end of us?"

I held my breath and waited for his reply.

"Yea," he laughed.

"Yea, that's the end of us? Or yea, I would

still be invited over?" I asked in a panic.

"Yea, you're still invited crazy," he said. "I'm pretty mature, I think I can handle that."

"Well, thanks that means a lot. I've thought about it a few times since we've been at it, but I'm not saying I've fully decided. It's just a thought," I said.

The first time I was celibate it was easy to be committed because I had such a strong vow tied to it. I had grown tired of sex, of the same men, and I wanted to wait for my husband. My mistake was that I had placed a certain value on one of my relationships. I thought he was my husband so initially I waited for him. I thought in the end we would end up together, but when it didn't happen I felt betrayed by the celibacy. I thought our love was invincible. I was a silly little girl then but my heart was in the right place. So with that, it is why I wouldn't want to declare being celibate again and give God anything less. I'm just an honest person. It may sound weird, but if I say I'm going to be celibate I'm going to do it with everything in me. How I looked at it, it was better to be honest with God than to lie to Him. Sometimes I would think about it and I would want to go back to being celibacy because I felt I had control. I didn't have to worry about messy emotions being tied to having sex and confusing me and the person I was having sex with. But in all honestly I was enjoying my sexcapades. So, it was for that reason that I didn't stop. I took the red pill because I wanted to see how deep the rabbit hole could really go.

I had drifted off to sleep, but I was

awakened by the sound of thunder. I wanted to wake Zay up, but I figured that would be rude after he had been working out and was probably tired. I cuddled next to him because it still made me feel safe. Before I knew it, it was morning and I was waking up again. Zay got ready for work and I made him breakfast. I ate with him and then I headed back to my place.

The event with our team was coming up and my braids had grown fuzzy. I knew it was time to get a new hairstyle. I cut the ends of my braids off one by one to get them as close to my real hair as possible. Once I did that I started to unravel them. Some of them seemed to just fall out. They were pretty chunky so it was easy to slide my fingers through them.

Once I got my braids down I headed for the bathroom and pulled conditioner from one of the shelves. I parted my hair in sections to make sure I got every strand. I loaded my hair with conditioner from the roots to the ends. I loved to get my fingers in my curly hair. I decided to let my hair soak with the conditioner in it all day. I got some chores done around the house and even handled a lot of calls. Some days I was on the phone all day without any new sign-ups. It was one of those things that happened in this business. Some people were eager to join but may didn't have the money that day so I had to contact them another day and some people just liked toying around and weren't interested in the business at all. This business reminded me a lot of the retail jobs I had held all through college in some ways. Retail had definitely prepared me for the no's of the world. Some people may want the $300 shoes and some may didn't. Some people may take you all around the store picking out items and get to the counter and have $0 or they had forgotten their wallet. In life, things happened but it's always up to you on how you respond to it. I kept a positive outlook because I knew that I would get those on my team whom I was meant to cross paths with. Some days I had so many sign-ups that I could barely handle and some days I didn't, every day I considered a new day to learn.

I had scheduled a hair appointment with my stylist, Tierra because I wanted to be in tip-top shape for the event. She was all booked up at the salon, but had agreed to come over to my house to do my hair instead. I liked this better because I could get all the deets in private. We had been cool since college so when we were together it was time for the girl talk reunion.

"So, what's new? Do you have a new boo or what? I need to know everything," I yapped.

"Girl, I am talking to someone new. Kenny and I didn't work out. We tried and we've been trying for too long, but I'm finally over it," Tierra replied.

"That's why I asked, you know I stay lurking and I noticed I didn't see any pictures of you two anymore so I had to ask. So what's your new guy like?" I asked.

"He's a really nice guy who I've known for

a while now so I just decided to give him a chance, but I'm happy I did. He's so sweet and and his head is the bomb," she started laughing.

"Well that's always a plus, so can I get a name?" I asked excitedly.

"Oh yeah, lol his name is Ralph. Girl let me show you his IG, he's so cute," she grabbed her phone.

Most of our visits went exactly like this. We caught up on gossip between each other and gossip about others.

"I feel like I know him or like I've seen him before," I pondered. "Oh yeah, he's friends with Zay. I saw him at the house the other day."

"Hold on, what? You and Zay? When did this happen?" she said with a shocked look on her face.

"Well, it hasn't been very long," I said.

I was really trying to take in the fact that her new guy was the one who gave me the weird look when I showed up at Zay's house the other day. Small world.

We chatted some more about her guy and then she spun me around and handed me a mirror. It was always so fulfilling to see the transformation she could do on my hair. I looked and I was loving my big bouncy curls. She could do a perfect install in an hour. She was amazing.

It was time for our big event and we had a lot of running around to do that morning. I was so happy I had got my hair done already and I didn't try to squeeze it in these few hours before the event.

Kara had on this very pretty white and gold shimmery crop top with tight fitting high-waist jeans and heels. Although, I never quite understood why she wore high-waist so much when her stomach was flawless. I guess it was more so for the fashion and not to cover her stomach like the rest of us. I wore a cute dress that came a little above my knees that had a cute flare to it. It was a rich peach color. I slipped my heels on and headed to start packing up all the items we needed. Kara and I got all the supplies together and started to pack the car. We had to get our business cards, clipboards for the sign-in table, pens, pencils, markers, and name cards for the prospects. We also grabbed the finger sandwiches, drinks, chips, and veggie dishes. Of course with all that we had to get plastic plates, cups, and napkins. Our uplines were basically doing the speaking and getting to our city. It was up to us to make sure all the other ends were handled because we were in the area already.

We got to the venue and set up everything. It was a very large room that we had paid for but it was going to be worth it. The food was off to the left of the room, the center was for all the prospects, and the right of the room was where all our business partners who didn't want to sit mingled at. It had taken a lot of preparation to get to this point, but I was glad the hard part was over for us. We just had to sit back and listen to our uplines repeat the same info we already knew and then add the new members to whomever was ready to be apart. So many people had misconceptions about network marketing so that was what most of the beginning was about. Everyone referred to it as the "Pyramid Scheme" without even getting full details. They referred to it as that and not realizing that even the largest companies have someone on top. The CEO, the President of the company, Regional Managers, District Managers, Team Leaders, Supervisors, whomever is above you that trickles down to the employee who is always on the bottom. That's a pyramid, but the thing about these pyramids is you'll rarely be able to work your way up to being in a higher position as fast as you can with network marketing. You literally make the rules. We had people in the company who in less than a year ranked in the 6-figure club or higher. It wasn't a "get rich quick" scheme or "Pyramid" scheme. It was simply a "Who's putting in the work scheme." What I loved about it was building the teams. It was easy to get 3 people on your team and for them to get 3 people and so on and so forth. Most of us had purchased from a network marketing company and didn't realize. It was the social media age; word of mouth was the best tool these days.

My mom had purchased from companies such as Mary Kay, Avon, etc. for years. Now, the body wraps, detox teas, etc. were all popular. These people all offered a person to be an independent sales person with their company. In addition, there were businesses like Costco and Sam's Club who offered memberships to clients. The only difference in our business was that our company paid us for sharing our membership information with other people. People made it hard but it was that simple. You could think of it as a referral program, but in life anything that wasn't normal kinda freaked people out. I admit, everything isn't for everyone but this was the perfect way to earn an income for me while I focused on my dreams.

Are you still with me? No, this is not a ploy to get you to be apart of some network marketing team I have. Can you try to keep up? I'm simply sharing what happened in my past. Got it? Good? Now where were we? The best parts are coming up. So now that you know what was being discussed at the meeting, I can get back to the story at hand. I just didn't want you guys to feel left out. :)

My upline was known for calling on me for stuff because I was such an amazing speaker. I guess it came from being an actress because it certainly wasn't my writing side. In fact, my writing side was my shy side. At times I wanted to just hide from the world and just write exactly what I felt. It was my acting side that gave me the confidence to speak and do it with a great personality.

I walked up and gave a small testimony on why I became a member. As always, it was to get the travel package, which I used often. It came in handy for discounts on hotels, flights, and vacation packages with resorts.

After I finished I joined the rest of the team that had gathered at the back of the room. Lennox and Zay were apart of this group along with some other guys. I had my eyes on Zay; he looked so handsome in his tailored suit. Yummy, I could just picture me eating him up. It's as if he was reading my mind because he walked over towards me. It just so happens I was standing by the clipboards that we were taking info on for the new prospects after we signed them up. We were keeping information for the newly signed and information because as always there were the ones who weren't ready that day.

"Did any of the people you invite decide to join?" I asked Zay.

"Yea, that's why I came to get the list so I could add them under my name," he replied.

"Oh that's wassup. Look at you making moves," I joked.

He looked me in my eyes and pulled on my skirt. I bit my lip and looked into his soul. I could tell we were going to have a good night. And then I got this strange feeling, it was as if I was being watched by someone else. I looked around the room, but no one was looking my way. I looked at the crowd of men who had huddled in the room like some animal pack, but nothing.

"Y'all did good tonight. I'm proud of y'all," Lennox replied.

By now all the guest had exited the room. We had so many people join that day so it was a success. Kara and I got the leftover snacks and things and headed for the car. It would come in handy for those moments where me or her was on a period craving in the late hours of the nights. As I was exiting the door, Zay saw me balancing the box with my heels on. He quickly came up to help me.

"Thank you," I said relieved.

"No problem, you should've just let me get these. I didn't know it was this much stuff left," he mentioned.

"Excuse me, is anyone going to help me with my box?" Kara demanded.

Zay was already headed towards the car. I hit the button to unlock it for him.

"I got you in one second Miss Kara," he placed the first box in the trunk.

He then came back to get the second box as Lennox was coming out of the door.

"Oh look who it is," Kara said.

She grabbed the box from Zay.

"I believe Lennox knows how to put a box in the car," she gave the box to Lennox and walked back inside.

"Feisty, lil' something ain't she? Just how I like 'em," he joked.

"TMI, Lennox. No one really cares what you like," I joked back.

"Don't even lie to yourself, you care," he said.

Lennox was always playing. I went back in to see if there was anything left but it appeared as if the two boxes we had was everything. Either that or someone else had already taken off with a box of snacks while we were away.

We all decided to go to eat at this nice Japanese place afterwards, called Osaka's
. It was the only thing we could settle on because

we had so many different eaters in the bunch. We had vegans, vegetarians, pescatarians, and your good ole meat lovers. Luckily, this place had a bit of everything so no one felt left out. I got my favorite chicken and shrimp hibachi with a small Japanese Bagel Roll, deep-fried. It was definitely to die for. We were all gathered around this large rectangle table that felt like something from Scarface.

"Do you know what you're getting?" I asked Zay.

"No, I don't really eat any of this stuff," he replied.

"Well fish is your favorite thing to eat and I'm sure there's fish on the menu," I insisted.

"Yea, it is, but I like fried fish and I don't see that," he said.

"Seriously, there's absolutely nothing else you'll even consider eating?" I asked.

"Maybe this shrimp hibachi meal will be ok," he said doubtfully.

"Well whatever you don't eat, trust I'll take it for you," I reassured.

The waitress came and took everyone's order down.

"I'll also have a Blue Dragon," Zay said.

"Uh oh, look at your being adventurous. I haven't even had that. Better be careful," I teased.

We all ate and before you knew it, it was time for the check to come.

"How do you want this split?" the waitress asked as she got to our part of the table.

Zay and I both answered at the same time.

"Two tickets please," I blurted.

"You can put these two on one," he replied.

Oh excuse me? How was I supposed to know that he was going to be nice and pay for mine? That was that independent, "I don't need anyone for shit" personality coming out. It's always nice when a woman can afford to pay for own and the guy knows that but he pays anyways.

Ladies, never assume that a guy is paying because believe it or not they're never obligated. Whether you're just fucking, dating, married, whatever. There's totally nothing wrong with going dutch or even paying for your mate's dinner at times

...but that's another topic for a different day. Right now, I was just smiling a bit because I just got my food paid for in front of everyone. Go Stori!!!

We had just exited the restaurant and I was headed to my car when Zay pulled me off to the side.

"Are you coming over tonight?" he asked.

"I can," I said as I gazed into his eyes.

"Oh, but I'll have to drop Kara off first. After that I can meet you at your place," I replied.

He moved in closer to me and held my chin.

"Or, Kara can just drive you car home and you can ride with me. I'll bring you back home tomorrow," he insisted.

His touch sent chills up my body and I could hardly speak.

"Well, well... that's fine too. I'll just go tell

Kara," I tried to get it out, but then he kissed me.

"I'm gonna go...I'll go...tell...I'm going now to tell Kara," I forced out the words.

It was just something about him that sent me into a frenzy. Did I mention that he was in a gray tailored suit that fit his athletic build to perfection? I couldn't stop biting my lip and fantasizing on how I was going to take it off.

Kara drove my car home and I got in the car with Zay. "Don't tell 'em" by Jeremih came on as we were riding.

"Oh, this is my junt," I started dancing and singing.

"Only it's you got me feeling like this, oooh why, why, why, why, why," I sang and rubbed on his face while he drove.

I liked riding with Zay; he didn't drive crazy like most guys. I didn't have to pull out the imaginary breaks from the passenger side. It was like a 15-20 minute drive from the restaurant to his house. Most of the drive consisted of me singing to him and him just laughing at me.

Once we got in the house I went straight to the bathroom located in his room. I could hear some music start as I sat on the toilet. I was hoping that it was only #1 and not #2. Although it is something that we all do, it is still awkward to do and I try to mask it anytime I have to. I was in luck, it was only #1. I washed my hands and entered into the bedroom. He had Trey Songz, "Trigga" playing and had turned on his red light. I could tell he meant business tonight.

I began to take my dress off and he walked

over.

"Let me," he unzipped my dress from the back and started to kiss me down my spine. His touch on my body was electrifying. I had never met anyone whose touch could make me numb yet I felt so awakened at the same time.

Awaken

They said he must be special to make you break in such a way.
I was bold, confident, and not looking for love.
Single, happy, and not even looking to play.
And then life hit me, as it always does.
I started to want, I wanted to indulge.
If I could ever find perfection in this human world,
it was plastered on your erection inside this broken girl.
Have you ever just wanted to kiss someone's tattoos?
Your body art, that moves with you,
so true, you do awaken me.
I'm quaking, I'm shaking, you're so elevating.
Control me, hold me, chaining.
Forever changing.
You're up then you're down.
The hardest to figure out.
We pray, you won't stay, you leave, you're back.
The cycle, you must break.
You can't push me away.
The feen, I'm in need, I'll plead,
I'll bleed, I'll die, if you leave.
You have awakened me.

I was just there, existing in his presence. The way he made me feel I didn't think I could ever leave it. I couldn't find a reason I would ever want to be anywhere other than with him. He lifted my leg in the air and stuck his tongue so deep in me as if he had a plan to touch my soul. A few movements of this and I was already gushing out all over him and he was gulping every bit of me. He then slid over to my clit and kept two fingers inside of me. It was at that moment that I realized he really had his entire face in it. I could feel myself starting to cum clitorally and I tried to scoot back up the bed, but he wasn't having it. He locked both of his arms around my thighs in the resemblance of a pretzel. I could not move and I was at the mercy of his tongue. I bellowed out and every bit of my juices came streaming out into his mouth. As my breathing started to slow back down I realized he was still there. He was still massaging my clit with his tongue and it was at this point I really tried to escape. I had never allowed anyone to stay there that long. Most times I ran from orgasms that seemed unfamiliar because it terrified me of how my body would react and that is exactly what happened. Before I knew it I was cumming again and this time was otherworldly. I literally felt my soul leave my body. I levitated, I fucking astral-projected. When I finally regained consciousness I knew right then I wasn't going to ever be the same when it came to him. I knew at that moment that he had unleashed some weird voodoo ritual on me that was going to have me doing dumb mess from here on out. I also knew that it was time for me to return the favor. I now was on a vengeance and I wanted ever so badly to snatch his soul from his body the same way he did me.

He was now on his back and I crawled in between in his legs. I bite his thigh just a little to cause a mix of sensations and then I kissed it. I worked my way to his penis while kissing and nibbling all over him. Once I got to the tip I swirled my tongue on his head then I popped my lips on it. I then began to lick on each side and I kissed it all over. I slapped his cock against my tongue and then I spit on it. I worked my way back up with kisses and then I took as much of it as I could in my throat. I realized his dick had a slight curve in it so it wasn't as easy deep-throating him as it had been for guys in my past. Nevertheless, I was still determined to please him. I started going as deep as I could faster and faster. I wrapped my hands around his cock and massaged it as I was swallowing him. I could tell he was liking it the way his body tensed up. I couldn't wait to take a load of him in my mouth, but then he started to move back. Apparently, he was ready to get inside of me now. I wasn't going to debate it because I was dripping all over his bed and was ready to have my holes pounded.

He was the best at what he did. I often wondered was he actually the best or was it just so good because he was the 1st person I had sex with after years of celibacy...nahhh he was just that good. It might've been a long time, but one thing is for sure I still remembered how bad sex felt and I surely could recognize good sex. Celibacy didn't change that knowledge.

As he was on top of me in missionary position I could feel him hitting my G-spot over and over. I was gushing out and cumming everywhere, it just seemed surreal. It was as if he was the God of Sex....

Sometimes I felt like our sex was so intense because he was the 1st guy ever in my life that I craved this badly, that I planned and found a way to get his attention, and to get him in this bed. I had never pursued a guy the way that I did him. And it made it all the more magical because he was worth it. He didn't just have mediocre sex. I'm referring to that kind of sex that you came off one time IF that. No, he had the type of sex that he didn't cum until I came and after that he still had a few good rounds left in him. I didn't just cum your regular one large one. I came multiple times and sometimes I was left shaking in the sheets for up to 5 minutes after he had stopped fucking me. Don't believe me ...then Google long orgasms. Ok, back on track. I'm getting turned on just thinking about it.

So after my body was drained of all life I just lay there in bed staring at the ceiling and then I noticed something poking me.

"Yeah, what's up?" I asked.

"We didn't pray yet," Zay said.

Pray? Why do we need to pray this time? After all the times we've had sex, why did he want to pray? Was the sex so good that he feels like he committed the ultimate sin? Are we praying to the same God? Or is this part of his sexual ritual and this is the closing part of the ceremony in officially taking my soul?

He got to the side of the bed and got on his knees and started praying. I got on my knees on the opposite side.

Now I lay me down to sleep, I pray the Lord my soul to keep if I should die before I wake I pray to the Lord, my soul to take...Amen.

That was the prayer I had said since I was a kid, I felt proud that I had remembered it all this time.

I opened my eyes and he was still praying.

I guess it was time for me to say my more adult prayer cause he was still praying. I figured he wouldn't be praying that long. Like really what do guys pray about? New Jordans? Ok, maybe that was a bit harsh he isn't that superficial and I don't think he even wears Jordans. Maybe he's asking for forgiveness. I wonder is he praying for me. I should probably pray for him.

Our Father, which art in Heaven,
Hallowed be thy name.
Thy Kingdom come,
Thy will be done in Earth,
As it is in Heaven.
Give us this day,
Our daily bread,
And forgive us of our debts,
As we forgive our debtors.
And lead us not into temptation,
But deliver us from evil.
For thine is the Kingdom,
The power, the glory, forever.
Amen.

I looked up and he was still praying.

I guess it's time for me to pray for my family members individually.

Then I felt the bed move, I opened my eyes and peeked. He was getting back into the bed. I decided to stay down a few seconds more so I could look like I was the one all into prayer. I waited a few more seconds and then I got back in bed with him. I snuggled up very close to him and smelled his aroma. His cologne mixed with his pheromones was just so comforting. I turned my butt towards him and he wrapped his arms around me.

He whispered in my ear, "Can you look at me for a second?"

I turned around and faced him. I could see the silhouette of his face from the moonlight peering through the window and the red light helped some.

"Yes sir," I tried my best to look in his eyes.

"I think I'm falling in love with you," he said.

"Wow, oh wow. Zay...really? Are you serious? Like you really mean that? Can I be honest? This is all so fast and I'm not sure where my heart is. I won't be able to know for sure until I can feel safe. You're popular, women love you, and you're beautiful. I don't know if our love can survive all that," I rambled without breathing.

"Slow down. You're thinking about it too deeply. It's no rush and I didn't tell you for you to say it back. I just wanted you to know. It's been heavy on me for a minute now and I just decided to say it," he said.

"Thank you, I'm really glad you told me. It gives me a lot to think about, but it also places things in perspective for me. I feel I was shutting down certain emotions because I didn't know where your head was," I said.

I snuggled back close to him and he weaved his legs in between mine like a pretzel. I felt safe with him. I felt at peace. I felt in love. However, that last part scared me so terribly. It just felt that in love just as perfect as everything is, it can be as hellish.

Chapter 3
<u>Official</u>

I woke up to a text message from
Zay.

Zay <3

Gud morning
beautiful.

> Good morning
> handsome.

What's on the agenda
for today?

> I'm going to lock down
> and get some
> writing done today.

Dat's wassup,
what you working on?

> A new book I've been
> jotting notes down
> for weeks and I'm
> finally starting.

I'm proud of you.
It's gon' be off
the chain I'm sure.

> I sure hope so.

I know it will.
I've read some

of your work,
you're really good.

                    Well thanks a lot Zay.
                    What about you?
                    Big plans for
                    today?

Yea a few actually.
My boy having a video
shoot today and he
want me to come hang
out in it.

                    Well your boy has
                    the right idea because
                    you're definitely eye
                    candy material. I'd put
                    you in a vid any day
                    just to look at that
                    body.

Lol, I don't know
about all that.
I think he just wants
his friends in
it. He's just getting
back in town. He
travels a lot. It's
kinda just the homies
kicking it.

                    Oh well, sounds

like fun. What time
are y'all shooting?

I'll be headed soon
because he wanna
get some good shots
while the sun
still up.

Oh yea, well now
is definitely a good
time to take advantage
of that natural
sunlight.

Well I'm about to
see what he's up
to and I'll get at you
later.

Ok, ttyl.

I decided that today I would stay in my
room and work on my writing. No going down to
Beale Street for drinks. But as soon as I said that...

"Knock, knock. Can I come in?" Kara
asked at the door all excitedly.

"What are you doing today? Don't you
want to go to Beale Street and drink Superman's at
our favorite spot and walk the strip flirting with the
tourist?" she begged.

"Well, I had decided that I was going to get
some work done today," I replied.

"Awww, work, smirk. Come play with me. You're always closed up in this room," she said.

"I am not. I'm always doing things for other people or taking calls. I haven't been writing as much as I need to and this book needs to get out," I said.

"How about if I leave you alone and let you write for a few more hours and THEN we go? That way you can work and play," she looked at me with the biggest smile and pleading eyes.

"That sounds fair. Ok, deal," I said giving in.

Kara came to my door with a cute red halter-top that was tied in the back similar to how a bathing suit is and some cute daisy dukes.

"You're all ready for a super seductive car-washing scene aren't ya," I joked.

I had thrown on a quick little dress that was flowy and allowed plenty of air in. It got pretty hot down on Beale Street in the summer and especially with 100's of people around. I was actually looking forward to getting one of our favorite drinks. It was a frozen drink that was red and blue with alcohol in it. The flavors were always meshed together really well and our girl Austin made them to perfection every time.

We parked at the Peabody and walked down to Beale Street. It was always optional to park closer, but that was only if you wanted to fight for parking. It was easier to just park somewhere and walk there from our experience. Although, if you went at the right time you could get lucky and get a side parking spot near one of the businesses.

We got to Blue's City Cafe and ordered our drink from the side window. It was exactly what I needed. It was the perfect summer drink to make you happy and cool you down at the same time. As always we walked the strip and laughed at the many drunk people making a fool of themselves. In addition, the culture was what we loved about Beale Street. Music just thrived there and not just the music that's out today, but that real soulful music. Live bands playing, lights flashing, the smell of history...ahh, truthfully there was no place like Memphis.

We walked for a while just looking and taking in the greatness. We passed by the Orpheum and FedEx Forum along our walk. We were just going where our feet led us. We finally made it back to where we started and sat down on the concrete near the Elvis Presley statue.

"I think I'm about ready to eat now," I said.

"Yea me too. What do you have a taste for?" she asked.

We could never really decide where to eat because all the food there was so delicious.

Pearl's Oyster House won this time. They had the most delicious seafood in Memphis. Kara and I both ordered a dozen of the Chargrilled Oysters.

"OMG, I never get tired of eating this," Kara said.

"That's what he said," I joked.

Kara started laughing.

"I kinda want to get some gumbo, but I

don't know if I'll have any room left after eating these crackers with the oysters," I said.

"Yeah, the crackers do help to get you full. These are the best freakin' oysters ever," Kara exclaimed.

"I always hate that we can't get them to go," I replied.

"Right," Kara gave a sad face and she continued to eat her oysters.

We went to Pearl's regularly and one time we asked to get oysters to go and it was when we found out the devastating news that oysters can't be ordered to go. From what we were told oysters have to be consumed within a certain amount of time or you could get severely sick. However, we didn't let that stop our oyster eating we just ordered as much as we wanted while we were there to get our fix.

We finished eating and got our ticket. We paid the bill and left our waitress a good tip. After that we headed back towards the Peabody to the parking garage. On the way we saw the regulars: a few homeless people, some girl who could barely walk in her stilettos, and a few drunk people barfing up their dinner.

"Ahh, gotta love Beale Street," Kara said.

I laughed. "I know right," I replied.

Kara and I rarely listened to music while we were in the car together. If we did it was a song out that we were crazy over. It wasn't that we didn't like music, but it was just that we always talked instead.

"Have you heard from Zay today?" Kara

asked.

"Yes, we text for a lil' bit this morning. He's doing a video with one of his friends or something. You know me, I stay outta the way when he's busy because that's what I be wanting when I got stuff to do," I said.

"Zay a model now? He does have the body though, so I could see why," Kara laughed.

"I don't even know which one of his friends calls themselves a rapper. I haven't officially met any of them I just see them when I go over to the house," I said.

My bed felt amazing when I finally got back home. The liquor was somewhat gone from eating at Pearl's but I could still feel it a little. Before I knew it I had drifted off to sleep.

It wasn't long before I was awaken by an incoming text message. I grabbed my phone and looked at the time. It was 2:00 A.M. It was Zay.

Zay <3

U up?

Yea, barely. What's up?

Still at this video shoot and I gotta be at work in the morning.

Oh well you better be leaving soon then.

I would but I rode here with them.

I could pick you
up if you want?

If it's not too
much trouble.

No, it's cool. I'll
probably just stay
the rest of the night
with you because I know
I won't feel like
driving back here.

That's fine.

Text me the address
I'm about to
get up.

I waddled out of bed and threw on a
spaghetti strap shirt and some cotton shorts. I slid
on my Converses and tied my hair up in ponytail. I
then grabbed my car keys and my crossbody and
headed for the door.

The location was right up the street from
my house. I was somewhat sleepy, but then I
became excited when I saw him standing out. It
was a really nice car parked in front of where he
was standing. It was a BMW I8 coupe, my dream
car.

*Now whoever was driving this could've
surely taken him home, but nooo let me wake Stori*

up out of her precious beauty sleep. I hope this wasn't a ploy to get some because I am going to sleep when I get to his house. Hmph!

I pulled up so that the passenger door was facing him and the parked car he was next to. He walked over and got in the car with me.

I then saw the other car window begin to go down and a guy stuck his hand out motioning for Zay to let his window down.

"Yea, what's up?" Zay asked.

"We prolly about to do a few more shots and then we gone head over to my crib. You think you'll be able to come that way tomorrow and do the last few shots there?" Kich asked.

I didn't look up to see any of his friends or the person who was talking. I continued to scroll on social media until they finished making their plans. But then I could feel that energy again. It was the same energy I had felt at the conference. It was if someone was looking at me...fixated. You know when your ears start to get warm and your face feels itchy because someone, somewhere is staring down your sideburns? I looked up but Zay had let his window up and so did his friend.

Maybe I'm tripping. I am exhausted.

I pulled into his driveway right behind his car. We both got out and headed in the house. I always liked being at Zay's house. It was very cozy.

I took my shoes off, my top, and then my shorts and climbed into bed. Zay headed to the shower.

I woke up with his arms around me. I was

happy he had let me sleep and didn't wake me up with a penis inside of me. That was some of the best sleep I had in a while. I noticed I had slobbed on his arm a little. I tried to wipe it off quickly but gently before he noticed.

His body was so heavy on top of mine but I loved it. He always curled up with me like a pretzel. One arm would be under me and the next would be around me along with his body coiled and twisted in between my limbs. I needed to use the bathroom but as always I decided to wait until he woke up. He was always positioned too perfectly for me to move him.

Zay's alarm on his phone began to buzz. I knew it was time for him to get up. I was somewhat disappointed because I loved being wrapped up under him. He must have been really tired because he didn't grab to turn his alarm off. I picked up his phone and got ready to swipe the bottom to at least stop the sound. When I picked it up I noticed it was actually someone calling. As I held the phone in my hand I read the name Niq at the top...

Call me crazy, but I'm pretty sure Niq is a girl's name. Probably short for some ghetto ass name like Shaniqua, Monique, Dominque, Janique, all of those names that someone's mom knew better than to put on a birth certificate.

Before I could finish my thoughts they were interrupted by an incoming text message.

Ohhhh, this bitch must really need some love and affection. The fuck? If he fucking another bitch then why that bitch didn't come pick him up.

Wanna wake me up out my sleep and shit like I couldn't have just stayed at home.

By now I'm looking all upside his head just waiting for him to hear this phone that was steadily going off. I finally got tired of holding it and I was two seconds away from throwing it at his head so I just woke him up.

"Zay," I nudged him a little.

"I'm pretty sure it's time for you to get up and your phone keeps going off," I said irritatedly.

He opened his eyes slightly and reached for his phone. I placed it in his hands and studied his expression when he read the name. He immediately unlocked the phone and started to respond.

"Who's Niq?" I asked.

"Oh, she's just my home girl," he said nonchalantly.

"Sooo, she's just like one of the homies huh? How come I never see her over when you and your "homies" have all those get togethers? Was she there last night? Wasn't that you and your homies too?" I asked sarcastically.

"Look it ain't nothing like that," he locked the phone back and got up. "I'm about to start getting ready for work. Don't you want to talk about something else now?" he asked.

"Nope, actually I think I just wanna go home," I started to put my clothes on.

"Oh what, you mad now?" he asked.

"Hell yeah, I'm mad because I don't believe you," I exclaimed.

He walked over towards me.

"You already know you the only person I'm feeling so that should be enough. Don't get worked up over nothing," he hugged me.

I decided to rest in that comfort and just believe it for now.

I sat back down and we chatted while he got ready for work. We both left his house at the same time.

My day was filled with errands and network marketing. I couldn't wait to get back home to take a relaxing bath. Kara and I pulled up to the house at the same time.

"Hey booski, where you been?" I asked Kara.

"I should be asking you that. You dipped out over the middle of the night and I'm just now seeing you," she joked.

"I've been back home since then, but you weren't here miss thang," I replied.

We sat down on the couch once we made it in the house.

Kara headed towards the kitchen.

"Wine?" she asked.

"Uhhh, girl you know it," I said. "Today is definitely a wine kind of day."

"Long night?" Kara asked.

"Well no, I actually slept really well at Zay's but I've been running a lot of errands today," I replied.

"Is that all?" Kara asked.

"Well and something did happen at Zay's today that has been on my mind also. I don't want to make a big deal about it, but you know how you get that feeling that something just ain't right?" I asked.

"Girl yes, that female intuition always be blinking," Kara laughed.

"Yes, that's what it is. It's like although he told me it was nothing and that I shouldn't be reading all deep into it, I can't help it," I said.

"Well, what exactly happened?" Kara asked.

"This morning some chick named Niq was calling and texting him back to back, but he claims she's just one of the homies," I said.

Kara gave me a side-eyed look.

"Exactly, my point," I replied. "But it ain't really anything I can do except keep my eyes open and attach the clues if something else does come up," I said.

I had been looking forward to the weekend. Zay had invited a lot of us over to a cookout. It was some of our business partners and just friends. Kara was my guest. I was happy she could come because I didn't know if I was going to see Niq or not. I wasn't looking for drama, but I just was preparing my mind in case I saw someone pushing up on Zay.

Zay's house had a really nice backyard that was perfect for a cookout. I parked on the side when I pulled up. It was already getting crowded and I was somewhat early. Zay had called and asked me to get the paper plates etc. because they didn't have enough. I could already smell the food on the grill as I was getting out of the car.

As we were walking up someone was

already holding the door open so we just slid on in. I saw Zay over in the kitchen doing something so I walked over to him.

"Where do you want me to put these at?" I asked him.

"Awww man, when did you get here? You slid in like a ghost or something," he joked.

"I just got here," I replied.

"My bad beautiful ladies, but this a man's thing today. Y'all are more than welcome to take your place back in the kitchen tomorrow," Tony, one of Zay's friends, joked.

"So you just gone do us like that?" I asked.

"For all I care y'all can cook everyday," Kara said.

"Right," I gave Kara a high-five.

"Aye, man lay off my girl," Zay replied.

His friend grabbed a pan filled of seasoned hamburger meat and headed back outside.

I got closer to Zay.

"Oh, I'm your girl now huh? When did I get the promotion? I didn't get the memo," I said.

"What's understood don't have to be explained right?" then he kissed me on my forehead.

I blushed and smiled at him.

"Y'all are welcome to hang out anywhere in here or kick it outside. I gotta go help them finish grilling," Zay said.

"Ok, we'll probably get some drinks and just kick it. Thanks bae," I flirted.

"Well he seems like he's shutting down all your negative thoughts today," Kara said.

"I guess so," I replied.

And then there it was...that burn against my face. I looked around as soon as I felt it this time. But still I could find no one who was staring at me.

"I have really got to stop drinking," I said.

Kara was laid out across my lap on the couch.

"Why would you ever want to stop doing that?" Kara asked.

"Just talking girl, but I do feel like I be tweaking," I replied.

The cook out started to die out as it got later. Zay came over and sat by me.

"Are y'all staying the night?" he asked.

"I sure don't feel like driving and I can't ask Kara what she wants to do because she's already knocked out," I said.

"I can give her some cover and she can just stay right here. Y'all don't have to leave," he replied.

"Ok, well it sounds like a plan," I said.

I walked back to Zay's room and got in the shower. I walked out with wet hair and wrapped in a towel. Zay was just watching me.

"Come here," he said.

I walked over slowly to him. He pulled me in closer and started to kiss me. Then he moved to my neck and started to lick and suck it. I started to lightly moan out. He pulled a condom out of his pocket and pulled me on top of him. It was too much to handle on top at first. I felt like I was just sitting up there for 5 minutes trying to wiggle and get it to go down. Being on top of Zay always took some maneuvering it was like my hole was just too tiny for his big ass dick to fit in. I finally relaxed and slid down on it. The more I shifted up and down the more comfortable it became.

"I love having you inside of me," I said.

By now I was bouncing all over him and he was moaning out. Zay was never much of a talker during sex, but I could pick up what he liked by his body language. He gripped my ass as I continued to ride him while spreading my cheeks apart as he pounded upwards. It didn't take long and I was already cumming. He flipped me over and began to eat me out right after. The next thing I know I was already cumming again. He could do wonders with his mouth. He climbed on top of me and continued to stroke.

"Yes Zay, just like that," I said. "Oh yes, fuck me," I continued. "Deeper, go deeper baby."

I apparently thought he only had a small amount of penis that wasn't in me because when he went deeper I immediately regretted it. I thought it was going to come out of my mouth and I swear I felt something pop inside of me. Zay liked to lock my arms up so I couldn't move or block his strokes.

I was so weak from after a full hour or more with him. I was still on the bed trying to recover and Zay had went to the bathroom. He then came back in and turned the light on.

"I think you're bleeding," he said.

"What do you mean?" I asked and then I looked down.

I was indeed bleeding. I guess I really did

hear something pop.

Did he really pop my cherry? Ain't I bit old for that? It wasn't popped when I lost my virginity? Who gets her cherry popped at 23 years old, like really?

I jumped up, embarrassed.

"Where's your cleaning stuff, I'll get it up," I said.

"It's fine Stori, I got it," he said.

"No, I'll get it up," I replied.

"I have the shower running for you. I'll spray this down so it doesn't stain and go throw it in the washer. It's not a big deal ok. Relax babe," he walked over and kissed me.

It really did calm me down because I felt so embarrassed knowing I had messed his sheets up. I went and got in the shower like he suggested. By the time I came out he had replaced the sheets and covers and was lying in bed. Luckily, I always kept a pad or tampon on me for emergencies. I grabbed my underwear that I had worn over there and a pad from my purse. I walked back in the bathroom and put them both on. I just wanted to be sure that all the blood was out. This was new to me.

I came and I got on my side of the bed and just planned to sleep there without cuddling. I was going to put myself on punishment.

"Come here Stori," Zay started to pull me over.

I was resistant to move.

"Did I do something wrong?" he asked.

"No, you didn't do anything wrong. I feel

like an idiot telling you to go deeper and you did and I messed up your sheets," I said.

"That's not your fault, if anything I should be apologizing to you. You are ok right? Do you feel any pain?" he asked.

"Yes, I'm ok. I felt something at the moment but after that I wasn't in any kind of pain. I didn't know anything had happened," I told him.

I finally decided to move closer to him. He wrapped his arms around me and began to pretzel me. I felt special in that moment and I felt that what we had was real.

Chapter 4
<u>Red</u>

Kara and I were having movie night. These were the moments where we got our giant, fluffy, sleeping bags out in the living room. We would throw on our onesies and watch every movie that made us happy with tons of snacks surrounding us.

"How about *Not Another Teen Movie?*" Kara asked excitedly.

"Yes, I love that one," I replied.

"After that one we have to watch *After Earth* because you still haven't seen it," I said.

"Ok, ok," she said.

"Popcorn is ready," Kara said.

"Yaayee, bring it in," I exclaimed.

I then got a text message from Zay.

Zay <3

Hi.

"Put it up. No excessive phone chat during movie night," Kara said.

"I know, I know. The movie hasn't even started so I'll just respond really fast," I said.

Zay <3

Hi bighead, I miss
you so much.

Ikr, imy2.

Send me a pic.

(Picture Delivered)

Nice, I can't wait to
put it in my mouth.

Me 2.

> Babe, I'm gonna
> hit you a lil' later.
> I'm having movie
> night with Kara.

K.

> Love youuu <3

Ily2.

He's super short with his messages today.
When I logged back into my current
situation Kara was giving me the death stare.

"Are you finished caking yet?" she joked.

"Yes I am," I replied while rolling my eyes.

We laughed at all the funny scenes in the
movie and ate our snacks. I really did love
moments like these. It was much needed.

During a part where I knew all the words I
looked back at my phone to get another glance at
the photo Zay had sent me. I clicked on it so it
would open up entirely in the "Details" section and
not just the message thread. I was smiling and
biting my lip when I noticed my name wasn't at the
top anymore...Niq? I exited out of the message and
then went back into "Details". That's when it hit
me and I was enraged. He had sent me a
screenshotted picture and didn't even have the
decency to crop out the bitch's name.

Yes ladies, y'all better start clicking on that
photo and looking at it from "Details" you might
have a screenshot from an idiot too. I apologize if
this isn't the same on Androids. My research is
only valid for iPhone users at this time because I

have one. Oh, and don't get cocky just in case your man was smart enough not to send a screenshot pic. Apple also has this really nice feature that adds a date and a time to the photo. If he passes the 1ˢᵗ idiot test then maybe you can try this one to see who else getting the nudes besides you. (Fellas, women are trifling too at times so y'all better get up on game).

Getting the nudes test:

Save the photo you just received to your phone. Go to the photo and look at the top part of your screen. If that date is any other date than the day you are living in then sir or madame your significant other is sending them nudes across country to niggas and bitches other than you. Thank me later. Please don't fall for the "I just be taking pictures and not sending them" lie. Oh, ok.

P.S. I know a way around all of this but I ain't gone tell y'all. I like to see y'all get caught up. So either send current nudes or don't send them at all. We don't want your recycled nudes.

Zay<3

I thought you and Niq
Were just friends.
She's a "homie" right?

She is.

Well then why did
you send me a picture

79

that was a screenshot
of a photo you sent
her?

What you mean?

      I cropped the photo just enough to show the
photo of him but close enough so her name would
show up. Then I sent it to him.

See...

That's crazy,
I didn't even notice
that.
      No shit Sherlock.

So is she still a friend?
You send dick pics
to everyone now?

That pic old.

      This ladies is classic male syndrome.
Refusing to answer the question at hand but
stating new information to deter you.

See you wanna play
games and shit
and I'm not the one
for it.

You getting mad

80

off of something
old. Chill tf out.

Chill tf out? Don't
tell me what to do?
No, I'm not gonna
chill because you
said she was just
a friend when she
was calling back
to back like Drake
the other day.
Now I'm seeing you
done sent the same
girl dick pics and
you want me to chill?
Fuck that. Fuck
you too. Bastard.
Just quit texting me.
Lying ass.

Zay wasn't much of the confrontational
type so I didn't get a response after that.

It seemed that as time went on we both
allowed our pride issues to get the best of the
situation. I wasn't going to say anything first
because I wasn't the one in the wrong. He didn't
say anything either for whatever reason.

I logged on Facebook and noticed he was
active a few minutes ago. I wanted to say
something but I didn't want to be a sell out.

*Why should I have to say something first
when I'm not the one who messed up.*

I decided I would reach out to see if he wanted to talk about what happened.

Lying Dummy

Hi.

Hello.

You there?

Are you getting my messages?

So you're just gonna ignore me?

Is that how we're doing it now?

Did you block me?

Zay...

I'm sorry, I just wanna talk about this.

I guess I should call.
rings

That's weird. It's stopping after one ring every time. I think he really did block me.

I felt like I had walked into an ulterior world. How was he now ignoring me and I was

apologizing? How did he make me feel guilty? I
remembered he had just been active on Facebook
so I went to write him there.

Varus Xavier Phillips

So is this how it's
going to be now?

What you mean?

You ain't talking
to me?
Ignoring me?
Did I do something
to deserve this?

I gave you what
you asked for.

I never asked for
this, that's a lie.

sends screenshot

That's not fair.
When I said
quit texting me
I was referring to
that moment. Not
for good. And then
I've been trying
to text you and
you've been ignoring
me. So not cool.

I didn't get it.

I sent so many
messages I don't see
how you didn't
get them. Unless
you blocked me.

Yea.

So you did
block me?
Do you plan
on undoing that?

Yea if you
stop acting crazy.

*He sends me a screenshotted dick pic and I
have to act like I am in the wrong and play nice
just to get unblocked?*

I'll be nice.
Am I allowed
to text your
phone now?

Yea gimme a sec.

So I waited a minute and then I text his
cellphone.

Lying Dummy

So are we good
now?

84

Yea we good.

I've really missed
you.

I missed you 2.
You busy?
You should come over.

Sure.

*Now how hard was that? This is the Zay I
remembered. This was the Zay that I loved. The
Zay that paid attention to me.*

And when I say Zay was so attentive...good
God. If I bit my lip or gave an eye of passion, he
saw it. When the pheromones started swarming, he
smelled it. Every moan or gasp I made, he heard it.
My body would tense up, he felt it. And once the
levee broke and everything came gushing out, he
tasted it.

"You're so perfect," I whispered in his ear.
"You make my body feel so good. I love you," I
moaned.

I don't think I could ever get enough of
him. My body just obeyed him and he knew every
single way to make it submit. I really never wanted
this moment to end.

I lost count of how many rounds we went
that night. We both would cum and I would just
look over at him with amazement and admiration
feening for more. I was all over him. I was
impressed by how many times he could get it back

up.

"Ok, I don't think I can go again," I said.

"I didn't know you had all that in you," he replied.

"I should be saying that to you, at this point I feel like I'm just lying here and you're doing all the work," I laughed.

We just relaxed there for a moment. I had my head on his stomach just listening to the breaths he was taking. I wanted every minute of this forever.

I found myself about to dose off and was awaken by Zay shaking me.

"You sleep?" he asked.

"I think I almost was, but not quite," I replied.

"I was going to tell you to get in a more comfortable position because you were hanging off the bed," he laughed.

"Oh, you're right. I probably should do that," I said.

As I moved up planning to get at the top of the bed I noticed Zay had gotten on his knees. I always felt like such a heathen when he was down there 1st and I was headed to sleep. I crept down beside him and said my prayers too. Tonight I kept it short because I was tired. At this point I felt like I didn't need to still pretend my prayers were as long as his to make a good impression.

I climbed up and made my way back in the bed and sank into the covers. I loved to look at his red light that barely lit the room. It allowed the perfect amount of light and the perfect amount of darkness. Then the coolness of the air blowing through the room and engulfing between the covers was so calming. I loved the feel of the cold, softness against my warmed skin.

I woke up the next morning and the sun had barely come up. I stared at the faint light coming through the window and then I looked at Zay. He was still knocked out. I moved in closer to him and buried my face in his chest. I stayed there for a moment and just inhaled his aroma. I kissed him there softly. I decided I was going to get up and make breakfast, but I couldn't move just yet. It was something I loved about lying there with him when he was so at peace in his sleep. It was something so beautiful about his sculpted body being next to me. It was like my private art show that was only for my viewing. I just wanted to stare and fondle him a little while longer.

Once I had got my feel in I eased out of the room in one of his shirts and into the kitchen. I wore a shirt just in case one of his homeboys had stayed over. He had a roommate who paid rent and then also an extra guest room. The guest room people didn't pay rent of course. Sometimes people would crash there if it was a long night and they couldn't make it home. Sometimes I think people just stayed over because Zay always had everything you needed at his house and it was just good vibes everywhere.

Zay's kitchen was normally stocked with food so I was sure he would have something I could whip up for breakfast. I opened the fridge and I found some bacon, sausages, eggs, and pancake mix. That was good enough for me. I checked to make sure there was some syrup somewhere before making the pancakes. I found an opened bottle in the fridge and an unopened one in the cabinet.

I whipped breakfast up pretty fast and walked it back to his room. I had poured him a glass of orange juice and water to go with it. Zay had these pop up tables for eating that were perfect for breakfast-in-bed. I set the breakfast on the dresser while I got the table up. I then moved it close to the side where Zay was still asleep. I couldn't believe that he had slept through all of that. I had fondled him, grinded on him, and went and clashed pots and pans together and he still hadn't woke up.

I got back under the covers and crept up behind him to see if he had started to wake up.

"Zay, get up and eat your breakfast," I said.

"I'm up," he replied.

"I can't tell. It looks like your eyes are still closed," I said.

"I been up for a minute, just laying her thinking," he said.

"Anything you want to talk about?" I asked.

"Naw, it's not a big deal," then he got up and turned towards his breakfast.

"Thank you," he kissed me on my forehead.

I think those were my favorite kisses ever. I felt like I had done a great job whenever I had received one of those. His kisses were the best to me.

We sat there after eating our breakfast and laughed and just talked about a lot of things.

"I hope we can keep this energy. I don't like when we're not talking, it feels weird," I said.

"Yea I agree, we gotta do better," he said.

"We will do better," I started laughing.

"We gotta speak it into existence," I said.

"Right again," he said.

"We will do better," he said.

We stayed in the house that day watching movies and enjoying each other's company. It was the best make up I had ever had.

"I think I'm getting hungry again. It's your turn to cook," I poked him.

"Oh is it, sure. What kind of pizza do you want?" he asked.

"You joking, but I'm actually down for that," I replied.

"Sausage and Pineapple, please kind sir," I said.

"I think I want pepperoni," he said.

"I'll just order them both. I think it's a deal for 2 medium pizzas right now," he continued.

"Pizza and wine sounds fabulous to me," I said.

We sat up and ate until we were both full.

"I need to workout now," Zay said.

"Oh here you go. Can't you just enjoy being normal and pigging out for one day?" I asked.

"Nope, it doesn't feel right if I don't work out," he said.

"Well now you're making me look bad," I

said.

"I guess I can run on your treadmill while you lift weights," I continued.

"That would be cool," Zay said.

So now our party was moving to Zay's small gym in his house. He had just enough equipment to sustain you just in case you didn't feel like going to the gym. I ran for like 20 minutes and called it a night. It was getting late and for some reason I didn't feel the day was over. Zay didn't have to go in until later the next day so I decided I would stay another night.

"I'm about to go take a shower. I'll see you when you get finished," I said.

"Ok, I'll be back in there when I finish this last set," he replied.

"Ok, well take your time because I sure am about to in this shower," I said.

I turned the water on and just watched it as it began to steam in the tub. Then I started the shower. I took off my shirt I had thrown on, grabbed some towels, and stepped in. It felt good just letting the water run over my body. I began to work up a lather of soap on my towel and washed my body. I got it super soapy and wet then let the suds roll down my back. Then I heard a door open.

"Zay, is that you?" I asked.

"Yea, I'm just grabbing a towel to wipe the sweat out of my eyes," he replied.

I got out of the shower and dried off. I figured I would grab another one of Zay's shirts because the clothes I wore over were dirty and I didn't feel like washing.

I came out in my towel.

"Am I allowed to steal another one of your shirts?" I smiled.

"I think I'ma have to make you work for this one," he said and grabbed me on top of him.

"Is that so? Don't be tryna grab me and you all sweaty," I laughed.

He started kissing me all over my face.

"Ill, cooties," I yelled.

"Get off me then," then he flipped me over.

"Punk," I joked.

"Guess I'll go take a shower too," he said.

"See ya stinky," I said.

"I see you still got jokes," he said.

"But wait come here before you go," I said.

"I want another kiss," I continued.

He leaned in and we started kissing.

He was sucking on my tongue. I bit his bottom lip. The kisses started to get so sloppy it wasn't even routined anymore. At this point we were just sucking on each other's mouth and trading saliva. I started to calm back down and remembered he was headed to the shower. I slowed my kisses up so I could speak. I spoke in between kisses.

"I guess I'll let you go to the shower now," I said.

He just kept kissing me.

"Or not," I said.

He started to unravel my towel and started to caress my boobs.

"I love you Stori," he said.

"I love you too Zay," I replied.

He kissed me on my neck, then on my lips, then on my nose, and finally on my forehead.

"I'm gonna go take that shower now," he said.

I was still sitting there with my mouth open. Gosh I was ready to swallow him whole, but I always respected his wishes and let him lead.

We slept that night peacefully and just cuddled. I appreciated nights like this.

I woke up the next morning and headed back to my home and he left for work.

"Karaaaaa, where are you?" I rushed in the house looking for my bestie.

I swung her bedroom door open with all my might and ran to jump on her. I started humping her leg like a dog.

"Didn't you get enough of that while you were on your hiatus from home," Kara joked.

"I think I did or maybe not," I rolled over and got the spot next to her.

"I've missed you chickadee," I said.

"I missed you too big head," she replied.

"So what have you been up to?" I asked.

"Absolutely...nothing," she replied.

"Do you know how amazing that feels?" she asked.

"I'm sure it was awesome," I said.

We chatted for a while just catching up. Then I started to scroll on Instagram.

"Oh gosh, this must be the video Zay was in," I turned the sound up on my phone.

"He looks good in this," I said.

"Who's the friend that's the rapper?" Kara

asked.

"Umm, it says Kich Mawni," I said.

"Oh, I think I've heard of him before. He has a few songs out that I've heard on the radio," Kara said.

"Sounds good. I think I like it," I said.

"Or maybe you just like how Zay is looking in it," Kara said.

"Well that could be a very big part of it. He is my favorite eye candy," I laughed.

I started to read the comments underneath the video.

View all 5 comments

traciee2bad
looking good
sosa_king5185
I c ya
therealestc2x
This junt fire.
baddieniq2u
Bae killed it.
cremedelacreme
saucy

If you've been paying attention then you know who was the 1st name I clicked on. Let's see what baddieniq2u looks like and see what juice I can find from her page, shall we?

I clicked on baddieniq2u's page.

Figures, she's not that cute. Oh, but look she has a big butt. Don't they always?

So, what does she do for a living? Thot.
I laughed.

"What are you over there looking at?" Kara

asked.

"Girl, I think I done lurked up on Zay's little friend page Niq," I said.

"Oh gosh, you done found that girl," Kara started laughing.

"I wasn't even trying, but she wanna be up under this video calling somebody "bae" and ish," I said.

"He can't be "bae" too much as much as I'm always around but I guess. She can have fun in the comments basic ass," I laughed.

"Let me see," Kara grabbed my phone.

"All she has is a big butt. Like why is that the girl guys always giving attention?" Kara asked.

"Girl your guess is as good as mine because seriously are they licking the ass and fucking it too?" I replied.

"The majority of guys ain't licking ass and girls barely out here taking it in the ass so what is the fascination?" Kara continued.

"I think it's just the look of it jiggling or maybe it's fun when they're hitting it from the back," I said.

"Maybe, but gosh how can they just ignore the face like these girls be hit!" Kara said.

We both started laughing.

I ended up falling asleep in Kara's room. Then I was awaken by the most horrible cramps ever. I went to her bathroom and checked to see if I was coming on my period. There wasn't anything in my underwear, but I did see a little something when I wiped. I eased out of Kara's room so I wouldn't wake her and headed down the hall to my room. I knew it would be better to go ahead and prepare because Aunt Flo was coming.

I got to my room and went to the closet in my bathroom to get a pad. I got one of my fluffy, comfortable ones that I liked to sleep in and put it in my underwear. After that I crawled under my covers and sunk into the sheets and pillows all over my bed. Then I heard a vibration on my phone. It was Zay.

Lying Dummy

I love you.

I love you too.
That was random,
is everything
ok?

Yes, you were just
on my mind.
I'm headed to bed now.

Me too, I woke up to
do something.
Goodnight.

Goodnight.

I probably should change his name back to Zay from Lying Dummy now.

The next day Kara and I went for a morning run. It always helped with my bleeding and cramps to get some type of exercise in. We loved to run down in Harbor Town because it was so serene. The Mississippi River was so beautiful under the bridge that connected Memphis to Arkansas.

"It always feels so good being out here," Kara said.

"Yea I know right," I replied.

"I love that even when it's hot outside it's still cool down here by the river," I continued.

We finished our walk up and headed back to the house.

I got in the shower as soon as we got in and then afterward I took a few business calls to add some people to the team. In between time I decided to go to IG to see what little miss "baddieniq2u" was up to.

I rolled my eyes as soon as I got on her page looking at her profile pic.

Really? Why do girls always do this backwards pose with their butt all out and looking like they neck broke turned around to see the camera? Anyways...

Then I saw it...

And why does she have a picture of her and Zay up? Let me guess. #MCM?

I started to read the caption as I continued rolling my eyes in disgust. I could feel my blood starting to boil at the thought of her even having a picture of my man on her page. I took a deep breath as I prepared to read the long caption attached to the photo.

baddieniq2u

#MCM goes to this guy. Well what can I say? We been going tough for like 2 years now and even tho we have our ups and downs this forever bae.

My headache and my heartbeat.

Headache and heartbeat? Oh it's about to be some headaches and heart attacks in this bitch when I'm done cutting up.

I called Zay so fast that I don't even remember going to his name in my phone. I sat there waiting for him to answer and didn't even realize he was at work.

Zay <3

You need to call me
ASAP.

I can't I'ma be
caught up
for a while.

You're fucking right cause you're sure as hell caught up.

This is important.

Well just text
it to me.

No.

Well gimme like
10 minutes
and I'll try to
call really quick.

Ok.

I was planning exactly how I was going to go in. Where should I start? Should I go straight

97

for the sloppy booty bitch or give him one last
chance to say if she was a friend or not? Naw, I'm
going straight for the kill. Bastard.

Then my phone rung. I took a breather and
answered it.

"Hello."

"What's up?"

"So you and Niq...y'all a thing now? Or
should I say y'all been a thing?"

"What you talking about mane?"

"I'm sure you know what I'm talking about
you got the tag."

"Tag? What tag Stori?"

"The one on IG. Please don't play dumb
now."

"Mane I know you ain't calling me off no
social media shit. You need to gone with that."

"Do I? You done told me how many times
that it ain't nothing? She a friend. Then why the
fuck is she on IG talking about bae this and that?
Talking about y'all been down? Like how long
have y'all been talking seriously? I'm tired of you
lying about the shit like keep it 100. You niggas
always talking about how real y'all is, but you lie
every chance you get."

"Mane I can't control what she says on her
page. Have I said anything? No, well that's your
answer."

"That's a cop out. You don't say anything
about me on your page either so what the fuck that
mean?"

"Well maybe that's your answer. I didn't

sign up for this shit."

"Fuck you and I mean that."

Then he hung up.

Oh he got me fucked up if he thinks this is
over.

Zay <3

Oh let me change this name ASAP.

+1 (901) 000-7684

Yea, that's better.

So you just gone
hang up on me?

I said I had
10 minutes.
I gave you 15.

And I wasn't done.
Like I just
need you to keep
it real with me.
All this lying
just making it worse.
I ASKED you
how many times
if this was what
you wanted to do
and how many times
did you say YES?
You could've left

me where I was.
I was cool with
our arrangement
but you started with
all that love shit.
Was all this just
a game to you?
I told you from
the jump that you
never had to lie
to kick it with me.
I wanted honesty,
I never wanted
your lies. I'll take
the bitter truth
over a sweet
lie any day. Was
all this just to
keep having sex
with me when
you wanted?

I'm busy.

You ain't shit.
I mean it
this time.
Delete all my shit
and don't contact
me again in
your worthless life.
Go play those games
with someone else.

I deleted his number, his thread, and any photos that I had in my phone. Well I did email the cutest ones to myself before doing that, but you get the picture.

The days began to pass and seemed as if they were fading right into each other. I told myself I was going to hold my ground this time and not give in so quickly. I did for a while, but as the days started to go on I missed him more and more. It started to hurt because he hadn't contacted me yet and I feared he had forgotten me. I started to feel like he didn't care anymore and feel as if he had never cared at all. I tried to put on a good face in front of Kara as if I was totally over him, but it hurt so bad.

The pressure started to build up and I felt like I was carrying the stress of the world. My act was starting to fade because I found myself reflecting on moments with him and tears falling at random moments. It was at these moments that I realized I should have had a back-up plan.

"How you been doing? I feel like you haven't been coming out of your room and you've been very distant," Kara said.

"I guess I've just had a lot on my mind. It's nothing personal," I replied.

"Well I didn't feel like it was towards me, but I know you and Zay have stopped talking. I don't want you sitting in your room all depressed over a guy," Kara said.

"I'll be ok," I replied.

"Stori, you don't have to keep up a face

with me," Kara replied.

"I know I don't. I'm ok, really," I said again.

"Well in that case get dressed. We're going to dinner at the Majestic Grille," Kara said.

She knew that was one of my favorite places to go eat. I loved that I could eat delicious food and watch an awesome silent film while doing it. It was like our twist on movie night and sharing it with others.

I loved the ambiance in the restaurant. It was the perfect thing for my break-up blues. We got seated at our table and told the waiter we would start with water to drink.

"On second thought, I think I need a glass of wine too. It has been one of those weeks," I said.

"Well get whatever you want, it's my treat," Kara replied.

"Oh really, I thought you brought me here like usual and I was covering my own tab. BUT, since you brought it up, don't mind if I do," I said.

"I'll have the most expensive thing on the menu please," I joked.

The waiter came back and we placed our order. I got the Cajun Chicken Eggrolls and Kara got the Famous Grilled Cheese. When her's came I had to get a bite because it was one of my favorite things on the menu as well. She also got one of my eggrolls. We always shared food. It was our way of getting a taste of more than one thing from the menu.

"This wine is awesome with this," Kara

said.

"Girl wine is awesome with anything. Wine is just awesome," I laughed.

A few glasses in and I had braced myself to text Zay. I didn't know if he would respond but I was going to give it a try.

+1 (901) 000-7684

Hi

Sup

How have you been?

Good, dealing with
the new changes.

Oh, I've really missed
you.

Oh yea.

Yea I have. What are
you doing tonight?

Probably about to go get
something to eat. I just
got off work.

Well maybe I can
come by later when I
leave from here.

I'm not there.

Oh you're not in
Memphis? I'm confused.
You just said
you were getting
off work.

I work in Ohio now.

Ohio? So you live
there now?
When did you move?

I got offered the
job last week
and I decided to
go ahead and
take it this week.
It was a good
promotion.

Wow, congrats.
You deserve it.

Thank you.

Well I'm out with
Kara at dinner,
so I guess I'll
just talk to you a
little later.

K.

I felt it coming, and I was trying my best to hold them back.

"Are you ok?" Kara asked.

"Yeah, I'm ok," I said as tears began to fill my eyes.

"Stori, what's wrong," Kara asked worriedly.

"He's gone, he left me," I replied as the tears kept falling.

"Who left Stori?" Kara asked as she rubbed my back.

"Can we get our tickets? I'm ready to go," I said.

"Yeah, I'll go up and tell them I'm ready to pay," Kara said.

"Thank you. I'm gonna head to the car," I got up and exited the restaurant.

Kara caught up to me and we walked the rest of the way in silence.

When I got in the car I let it all out.

"How could he move and not even tell me bye?" I asked.

"Am I really that bad? Were we really that bad?" I continued.

"How did I ever confuse what we had for love?" I said in between each gasp of air I took.

"Stori, he's dumb and he doesn't deserve you," Kara reached in to hug me.

I placed my head on her shoulder and wailed my eyes out. My heart hurt so bad. I couldn't believe he was treating me like someone he didn't know or never cared for. Everyone knows it's common courtesy to say goodbye to someone.

The next few weeks were all a blur. I believe I slept through most of it. I couldn't even go in the group chat for days because it hurt every time I saw his name pop up.

As time went on I figured he had started dating someone new because the messages I sent didn't even get replies anymore.

+1 (901) 000-7684

Hi

Zay?

Did you get a new number?

What did I do to make you treat me like this?

You told me you loved me... where is that Zay at?

Good morning.

Are you just busy getting settled?

I'm praying for you.

I know
there must really
be something wrong
or going on with you for
you to be acting like
this.

Good night, don't
let the bed
bugs bite.

I hate that I will
always love you.

This is my last
message. I won't
bother you again.

I really miss you.
Will you please just
talk to me?

Zay...please talk to me.

I passed your house today,
it seems weird not
to stop by.

I guess you blocked me.
I don't know why.

Do you have girlfriend
up there now? Is this

what that's all about?

I'll be in Ohio for
a few days
on business. It'd be
nice if I
could see you.

At this point you would think I had given up and lost all hope. I didn't and I couldn't. I kept holding on to the better days and blaming myself for the last thing I said to him.

You ain't shit. I mean it this time. Delete all my shit and don't contact me again in your worthless life. Go play those games with someone else.

I kept feeling like if I had not said it we wouldn't be here. He would've told me he was leaving and we could have had a long distance relationship.

It was all my fault. I'm so stupid. I didn't even have to go that far. I didn't even have real proof of him having a thing with that girl.

It was as if my next phase after being hurt was conviction. I blamed everything we had went through on myself. I told myself I should have just shut up and dealt with it.

I have a horrible attitude. All I do is run people off just like Zay. I'll never have anybody genuine.

My thoughts were interrupted by a knock on the door.

"Come in," I said.

Kara came in and sat on the edge of my bed.

"Have you started dating anybody new yet?" Kara asked.

"No, I haven't. I'm not looking," I replied.

"Well you should be. I hope you're not still waiting for Zay to act right," Kara said.

"No, not really. I mean I don't like how things ended and I hate that he's mad at me. If I could just get some closure and get on good terms with him I would be better," I said.

"He's a jerk and you should just forget about him," Kara said.

"If only it was that easy," I said.

"Do you think you're really that into him or is it because he was the 1st guy you were with after being celibate for so long?" she asked.

"Yes I am. I've talked to other guys in between the time and they didn't capture my attention. It was just something about him and I can't let it go," I said.

"You're gonna have to let it go Stori or it's gonna ruin you," Kara said.

A few months passed and I started to live again. I got back on my normal routines and started back having business meetings with my team. Everything was looking up and I was happy again. I had found a way to deal with my life without Zay, but for some reason I still left a crack in the door. I still had my window opened just in case and that was my downfall.

I was scrolling on Instagram and I decided to go see what Zay had been up to. He didn't post pictures much but for some reason he still chatted with people in the comment section of his posts. I basically kept up with his life through that. I knew about his job, he just got a new place to stay, and so many other things. Today my eyes glimmered as I read one of the comments of some girl asking when he was coming back to Memphis.

It was on a picture of him at the gym.
View all 9 Comments
zayphillips
Go harder.
rastaprincessgold
Wud up stranger?
zayphillips
Nah that's you.
rastaprincessgold
I swear, you never answer your phone.
Oh, so I see it's not just me, hoe.
zayphillips
You haven't hit me up.
rastaprincessgold
That's a lie, when you coming back dis way?
zayphillips
I'm having my bday bash there.
rastaprincessgold
Oh word? I'm in dere.
zayphillips
You better be, bring your crew out too.
So he's going to be in Memphis...this month? I know what you're thinking...I shouldn't care and I should just leave him alone right? I did the total opposite. I went out and got him a

birthday gift. Everybody loves gifts right?

I went out that day and I decided I would get him a birthday gift. I didn't want to overdo it and because I didn't know if he had flown or driven here I didn't want anything too heavy if he was traveling light.

I kept it simple and got his favorite boxers and some sweat resistant workout clothes. I had worked in a gift shop before during college so I wrapped everything myself and made a beautiful red bow to go on top. Red was his favorite color. He finally posted a flyer about his B-day Bash and how to get in. His friend was a promoter and was selling the tickets. I decided to get tickets for me and Kara. I text the number on the flyer.

+1 763 888 9867

Hi, I'm tryna get a
ticket to the
event this weekend.

Ok, what part
of town are you
in?

I'm at Oak Court
Mall right now.

Ok, stay there I'ma
send someone
over there to give
you one.

Ok, cool. I sat in my
car and waited.

Then I got a call. It was Zay's number. I
answered.

"Yea, what part of the mall are you by?"

"I'm over here by the Dillard's parking
area."

"Ok, what you driving?"

*Did he really not know it was me? That was
kinda good and bad. Good cause it's not as
awkward for me now and bad because that meant
he didn't have my number saved anymore.*

"I'm driving a yellow Jeep Renegade."

"I think I just passed by that. I'ma drive
back around."

*Hmm...he must have a new car or he's in
someone else's car because I didn't see his car
come around.*

Then a black Camaro rode by me and
started to back up. I figured it was him. I took a
deep breath and braced myself for what was about
to happen. He started to walk towards me. He was
wearing a tank and those muscles were just oozing
out. I loved how his tattoos were placed on his
body. I was having the reaction I always had to
seeing him. It was like everything began to tighten
inside my walls and my heart rate sped up.

"Hey," I said.

"Stori? What's up?" he asked as he reached
in to hug me.

I melted right in my boyshorts when he put

112

his arms around me.

"So you tryna party huh?" he asked.

"Yea, I thought I'd come out. I decided to get tickets for me and Kara," I said.

"Oh cool, I'm looking forward to seeing y'all," he said.

"If I had more time I would say let's grab a bite to eat, but I gotta go drop off some more tickets," he continued.

"What are you doing after the party?" he asked.

"Nothing that I can think of," I said smiling.

"Oh cool, I might hit you up then," he said.

He gave me another hug.

"Can I text you now?" I asked.

"Or maybe I should ask... if you're going to reply if I text you?" I looked down at the ground.

"Yea I'll reply," he said.

"Ok," I looked up smiling.

He walked back to his car and I got in mine. I exhaled and was happy that it didn't end horribly. I text Kara about the party we were going to tonight.

Kara Poo <3

I hope you're ready bitch
cause we're getting
out the house tonight.

Oh gosh, where are
we going?

To a party.

Is it Zay's party
cause Lennox
is here for it?

Yes lol.

I don't condone this,
but hey I guess I can't
turn down a party.

Yay! Cause I can't turn
up without my bestess.

Yea, yea, you
always tryna
sweet talk me.

We got ready for the party in Kara's room.
"So you finally got to talk to the devil,"
Kara said.
"Kara, he is not the devil. Stop it," I said.
"I mean I don't know how else to describe
him. He sees that you had started doing good
without him and he slides back in," she said.
"Well he didn't slide back in I contacted
him," I said.
"He's allowing it. Y'all are back texting and
everything. He's like a drug and he just wants to
get you back hooked so he can..." she saw how I
was looking and stopped.
"Sorry," she said.

114

"No, it's ok. He's just using me so he can leave me again? Why do you think he'll do that?" I asked.

"Well I'm not saying he will, but it's starting to seem like a pattern," she replied.

"I wouldn't say that and each time we stopped talking I did tell him to leave me alone. I probably should just choose my words more carefully," I said.

"Well anyways, I'm ready to get this liquor in my system and turn the fuck up," Kara said.

We both had on our freakum dresses with heels looking amazing.

We made it to the venue and walked in. The party was pretty live. We got drinks and got a booth next to Zay's B-day booth. I didn't want to be right under him and we weren't on the best terms. Kara danced with Lennox a few times, but I didn't come in contact with Zay much. Every time I looked up he was surrounded by all his friends so I just enjoyed myself with other people as well. Besides I was going to see him tonight.

Kara and I left the party early because she had too many drinks and wasn't feeling well.

"You sure you gone be able to have Lennox all in your stomach tonight?" I joked.

"I'll be fine soon, trust me. I haven't seen him in some months so I better get well," she said.

"Are you seeing Zay tonight?" she asked.

"Possibly, if he isn't too intoxicated. Did you see all those drinks he was taking?" I responded.

"Yea he was throwing them back, but Zay

is a big fella so I'm sure he has a high tolerance," she said.

"He does, but he was drinking more than normal. They had a lot of bottles in that booth," I said.

We finally made it home after a few random stops of Kara having to puke on side of the road. When I got in my room I went in and took a shower. I text Zay before going to bed. I didn't get a reply so I didn't wait up.

I woke up the next morning and text him again.

Zay

Are you coming to get your gift?

I looked at the time and it had 9:15 AM. I figured that was why I hadn't gotten a reply yet. I continued to lie in bed for a while longer. Around noon I got a response.

Zay

Idk if I'ma have
time after spending
time with my fam.

It's cool Zay, well Idk
if I told you last
night but Happy
Birthday. Love ya.
That day was the 1st day I felt the change.

My heart had grown tired and I no longer could see the bigger picture anymore. He wasn't the person I thought he was and I was done.

Diamond
I stopped caring yesterday.
I deleted your thread.
I stopped caring yesterday.
I blocked your number like you said.
I stopped caring yesterday.
I quit reminiscing on the good moments.
I stopped caring yesterday.
I won't be on Instagram reading all your comments.
I stopped caring yesterday.
When I took that final blow.
I stopped caring yesterday.
No more making excuses for you.
I stopped caring yesterday.
Yes, I know you've been hurt.
I stopped caring yesterday.
I got mistreated for those scars and that's worst.
I stopped caring yesterday.
Maybe your boys can fulfill all your needs.
I stopped caring yesterday.
They always got more time than me.
I stopped caring yesterday.
You're stupid for throwing away a diamond.
I stopped caring yesterday.
You lost my value but I'll still have worth to the person who finds me.
I stopped caring yesterday.
I really did fight for this thing.

I stopped caring yesterday.
I'm so wounded I don't even want to throw
another swing.
I stopped caring yesterday.
Seems like I finally got the hint.
I stopped caring yesterday.
Only I still thought we were meant.
I stopped caring yesterday.
I'll cry about it tonight.
I stopped caring yesterday.
And in the morning everything will be alright.
I stopped caring yesterday.

Chapter 5
<u>Burning Desire</u>

The next few months flew by and seasons changed. I accepted what was and realized that it was time for me to move on. I wasn't the type to go looking for someone new but I knew how the Universe worked. In due time I got stronger and I didn't think about him nearly as much. One thing I was good at was suppressing emotions. It might wasn't the best way to cope but it was easier. I erased every thought of him and really stayed off his social media. K. Michelle's *Anybody Wanna Buy a Heart* was my venting album during this time. When I needed to miss him I could get it out and when I needed to say fuck him I could get that out too.

One night I was sitting at home and I really had a taste for Blue's City Cafe but Kara was out of town. I went by myself sometimes but it was always fun to be with someone else. I decided to write a status on Facebook to see if I could get a quick response from some of my friends in the area.

Vistoria Jefferson

Hey! Who's in Memphis? Anybody wanna go to Blue's City Cafe with me? Don't everybody comment at once lol.

I waited for a while but it seemed I was only getting likes. Then I got a response. I went to it. *Kich Mawni.* The name looked familiar. Then it hit me. This was Zay's friend...the rapper. I went ahead and opened the message completely to see what he wanted.

120

Kich Mawni

I wanna join you.
I feel like getting
out and turning
up a bit. I been
in this house
all day.

Blue's City Cafe
is a restaurant.

Oh well, it's still
on Beale
tho right?

Yes it is.

Well cool, we
can go there
later.

I might wasn't talking to Zay, but I wasn't
about to do some fucked up shit like this so I tried
to gain control of this conversation and steer him
another way.

You're a rapper right?

Yea I do a lil something.

I think I heard your
song on the

radio the other day.
I really liked it.

Appreciate it.

No problem.

So are we hitting
Beale or what?

You know I think I'm
going to just eat
here. I really
need to finish
writing.

Oh, you're a writer?

*Fuck, he totally missed my ploy to try to get
out of this conversation, and now he's starting a
new one.*

Yea, and I'm working
on an audiobook
at the moment.

Where you recording
at?

I haven't found anywhere
Yet but I know I
will soon. I'm trying
to get the content
down 1st.

I'm intrigued,
what else do
you do Miss
Vistoria Jefferson?

I do some acting
and video
editing as well.

Well I think we should
set up a business
meeting. We
may can join
together and
create some
stuff.

I'll think about it.

Take my number
down just in case.
I have a huge
studio that you
can record in
whenever you're
ready to start
laying your audiobook.

Wow, really? Thank
you! How much
would you
charge me?

We can talk
prices once you
text me.

Ok, I see.
Conditions.

I sat there for a moment and I questioned
where this was going.

*This is dangerous Stori. He already has
you laughing and that tingly feeling in your chest
is buzzing. You haven't talked to anyone since Zay
so your heart may be in full rebound mode but you
canNOT rebound this way. You cannot rebound to
one of his closest friends. He calls this guy his
brother. So you need to back away from Facebook
swiftly and let it go.*

And then she spoke. She counteracted
everything I had just thought.

**First off, I don't owe Zay shit. And
secondly, this is innocent. I will just be recording
songs. I don't know the future and who am I to
say he even wants me like that. Do it. Text him.**

I felt like those cartoons like I had a good
and bad side on me. And then I didn't know if the
bad side was really bad or was she just real.
Whatever she was, she won. I was curious. Doesn't
curiosity always kill the cat?...well meow.
I went ahead and saved Kich's number in

my phone and sent him a text.

Kich Mawni

Hi, it's Stori.

Hey beautiful. So let's
talk business. I believe
we can benefit from
each other's talents.

Hmm...possibly.
Continue...

I figure I can help you
with your audiobook
and maybe you
can help me with
some editing with
my videos. I have
a crew but it is times
that I shoot footage
myself and I'd
like if I could
have a beautiful
tutor to show
me how to use
my software.

Well that sounds
like a good
idea. I'm in.

No I'm not. Stori, take that back.
Yes I am.

So how about
we meet up for
a business lunch
tomorrow?

Sure, just tell
me where.

How about Frida's?

I love Frida's! I'll
meet you there.

So I had to tell Kara what was going on
because I was uneasy. I kept feeling like I
shouldn't go but then something was pulling me in
ever so deeply.

"I have a business lunch tomorrow," I said.
Kara was folding her laundry.
"With who? I'm glad to see you getting
back out there," she replied.
"Kara, I said business lunch not a date," I
said.
"Oh, if it's with a guy then it's the same
difference. He just used business date to make it
sound professional and not like he's tryna get some
ass," she laughed.
"Shut yo' ass up. Can I tell my story
please?" I said as I hit her with a pillow.
"Go ahead Queen Vistoria," she said.
"Well he's looking for some help with
videos and he said I could record in his studio," I
said.

"I see you steady avoiding the question I asked 5 minutes ago. I said with who?" she continued.

"It's with Kich," I said looking away.

"Kich? Kich Mawni? Zay's friend, Kich Mawni?" she asked.

"Yes," I said confidently.

"Well hell yea, that's what his ass get," Kara said excitedly.

"Kara it's not like that. I'm not going to get back at Zay. He made a really good business proposal," I replied.

"I say go and you don't owe Zay a damn thing," she said.

"Go and see what he's talking about. If it's just business then ok. If not, then ok. You're single and Zay ain't shit," she continued.

So since it was no longer just me and my battling consciousness that agreed I felt better having my bestie's approval.

I got a good night's sleep and woke up with much anticipation.

I text Kich as I was pulling up to the restaurant.

Kich Mawni

I'm pulling up.

Ok, I'm getting out.
I'll wait by the door.

Ok :)

I was somewhat nervous so I just reiterated to myself that this was a business meeting and it wasn't a date.

As I approached the door I could see Kich waiting.

"Hi...Kich?"

I asked because it was our 1st official time meeting and I didn't want to assume.

"Yes. I hope you're ready to eat I'm starving," he replied.

I stuck my hand out so we could shake, but he pulled me in for a tight hug. He smelled amazing. I felt a voltage; I backed away and studied this specimen. Kich had a very exotic look. He had these piercing eyes that seemed to speak to my soul. There was something mysterious yet luminous about him. His lips seemed to be sculpted onto his face. *Perfect.*

We got to our table and started to discuss our business plans. Somewhere along the way I felt Kich was giving me the eye so I made sure not to give direct eye contact. There's a certain energy that seems to release once you lock eyes with someone.

"So I'd love to also get you in a few of my videos because you're beautiful," he said.

"Thank you, I would like that too. I'm into all things entertainment," I replied.

"That's what I like to hear," he said.

"So when are you looking to get your audiobook out?" he asked.

"Definitely this year. I want to use it to tell

people other ways they can make money working from home," I said.

"Hustler, I like that. Well you can use my studio anytime you like," he said.

"Wow, thank you Kich. So is there a fee or anything?" I asked.

"No, there's no fee. I feel you have things I can benefit from and I have things that can benefit you. Think of it as a business partnership," he said.

"Ok, cool. I'm with it," I replied.

"So I say we get to work right away. You ready to get in the studio?" he asked.

"I mean, sure. In this business you gotta know when to jump on opportunities," I replied.

"My studio is in my house, is that ok with you?" he asked.

Now see this better not be a ploy to get me to your house and it better not be one of those garbage can studios. If it's gonna sound like I could have recorded it on my iPhone I"ll have to pass.

"Yea, that's fine. Even if I don't do any major recording today I still would like to check it out," I replied.

We got to-go boxes for the rest of our food and then Kich walked me to his car.

"You're coming by right now? Right?" Kich looked down at me as I was sitting in the car.

And it was the first time I looked up and I locked eyes with him.

Attraction

It's like when Jacob imprinted on Renesme,
see he has me.
And not just sexually,
like I'll do anything to be what he needs me to be.
I just wanna be his peace.
His Queen.
Jack-of-all-trades is he.
He has shifted all of gravity
and I am the soil of the seed
he planted in me.
When you start to understand the Universe
coincidences once dispersed are extinct.
So because of this, I knew we were meant.
He was my Dom and I was his Sub.
Harley Quinn to the Joker.
We make magic, Al Roker.
I am proud.

"You wanna trail me or you want me to text you the address?" he asked.

"Just text me the address in case something happens and I can't keep up with you," I replied.

I drove through an open gate that had a very long driveway. After following the driveway to its destination it led me to a house located at the address Kich had given me, but for some reason I felt I must have entered it incorrectly.

There's no way this is Kich's house. This isn't a house it's a mansion.

I looked around for anything that could give me a clue as to if I was at the right address. And then I saw a car pulling up in my rear-view mirror. It was the same black car with tinted windows from the restaurant. It pulled up near the front door where these steps were.

The house was sitting on acres of land. Gorgeous, green, grass just flowed all around it. It was a creamish-colored mansion that seemed to almost glisten like pearls when the light hit it. It reminded me of the house from Fresh Prince of Bel-Air.

Then it happened. Kich hopped out of the car and motioned for me to pull closer. I pulled my car right behind his. He walked up to the car and I let my window down.

"I mean were you planning to get some exercise in or something and walk a mile to the house or what? Why were you parked so far away?" he asked.

"Oh, I didn't see your car yet and I can't see in the car garage over there so I was making sure I was at the right address," I said nervously.

"Yea, you're at the right address. You coming in or what?" he asked.

"Yes, I am coming in," I replied. I frantically started to look for my purse all over the car.

"One second, I can't seem to find my purse. I hope I didn't leave it at the restaurant," I explained.

Kich leaned in through the window slightly and tipped his head over some. He smelt of the crispest cologne I had ever inhaled. It was like the best smelling chicken noodle soup on a winter night and you have a cold. I could sit here forever.

"Isn't that it under the passenger seat. I see

131

a string," he said.

I looked over at my passenger seat and pulled it from under.

"You're right, it is. Thank you," I said trying to sound confident even though I knew I was making a complete fool of myself. I put the car back in drive and pulled closer to the front entrance.

I grabbed my purse, let the window back up, and got out of the car. I hit my button on my keys twice so it would lock and set the alarm. I felt silly as he waited on the bottom step for me and I was wasting all of this time. I felt silly even trying to set an alarm as if anyone would want my Jeep after seeing this house. I just followed up the steps like a dog with its tail tucked. Part of me wanted to evaporate into little pieces now and never come back. Part of me wanted to imagine that this day had never happened and part of me wanted this day to never end.

As I entered the house a chill came over my body from the excitement of even being there. I would feel like I had made it if I lived there. The tall ceilings that I could never touch even if I was on a ladder. The huge windows that let vast amounts of sunlight in. He headed for the bar area and grabbed two glasses.

"You drink?" he asked.

"Yes, but I'm fine. I don't want anything right now," I replied.

He put the other glass back on this rotating glass display stand and proceeded to pour some type of brown drink in the glass. He sat on a bar stool and I sat on the nearest couch.

"You're very quiet, you weren't even this quiet at the restaurant," he said.

I finally mustered up some confidence to say what was really on my mind.

Which is shocking because I never have a problem saying what's on my mind. Actually I say it too much and it often gets me into trouble.

"Don't take offense when I say this but I don't really know your name as being a big time rapper so how are you paying for this house?...it's huge," I said curiously.

I just knew it. I had come to the conclusion that I was in some drug dealer's house. I bet he's like a King Pin. Good job, Stori. Good fuckin' job, Stori.

"Care to answer? Any day now," I said sarcastically.

"You've been in my house for all of 5 minutes and you are questioning me about my finances. There's ton of ways to get money in this world Vistoria without being known...as you say. The Universe has endless opportunities," he remarked.

"Hopefully, all legal," I commented under my breath.

"I've been to prison before and trust me I ain't tryna go back. It's all legal sweetheart," he said.

I looked away in embarrassment.

"Maybe you didn't find what you were looking for because you looked up Kich Mawni, the rapper, instead of looking up Kich Montel...the writer. Now that will probably give you what you're looking for," he remarked.

"Ohh...you're a writer. I didn't know that. I guess I'm learning new things about you everyday," I said.

I wanted to disappear. I really had put my foot in my mouth this time...or at least I should have put my foot in my mouth. I had just embarrassed myself in front of a well-paid writer. I was sure he had some dope connects to live in a house like this and I was sure he could help me way more than just allowing me to record my audio work in his house.

"Now you're sitting over there with this dumbfounded look on your face. I bet you feel like an ass now huh?" he joked and then touched on my face.

"Move Kich," I pulled away. I also tried to ignore this spark that just shot through my body as if he was an eel touching me.

I decided I should lighten the mood and start to talk about other things now.

"So Kich, where did the Mawni part come from?" I asked.

"Well isn't it obvious? Real name Kich and I love Mawni," he said confidently.

I sat there looking confused still trying to decipher what he meant. I even spelled the name out to see if I was missing something.

M A W N I ...Mawni?

"Money, mula, hell Nicki Minaj called it Muny and did anybody question her ass? Kich Mawni...Cash Money," he said.

"Umm, ok. I see it now," I said to reassure him. "Maybe I was just having a slow moment. It's very creative and Kich is a very beautiful name. I'm glad you kept it incorporated."

He started to walk closer to me and then he touched my arm. There was that eel again. It was a ray of electricity shooting through my veins but not in a painful way. It was sensational.

"And I also like to make women...mawn," that's the bonus part. Then he brushed his fingers across my lips.

"Kich, this is supposed to be strictly professional. You know I dated Zay. I can't go there with you," I scooted farther up the couch.

"You talked to Zay?" Kich asked.

"Yes, didn't you know that?" I asked.

"I mean Zay has a lot of girls it's hard to keep up," he smirked.

I looked away as if that didn't just take a stab at my heart.

"Right, I shouldn't have assumed you knew," I said.

"Well Zay is a lucky guy, I wish you too the best," he said.

"Thanks. You know I believe I should go," I said as I grabbed my purse.

"You don't wanna at least check out the studio?" he sounded disappointed.

"No, I just don't know if this is going to work Kich," I replied.

"I will behave, hey this is professional. I crossed the line and I apologize," he said.

"No, I feel like me coming here crossed the

line. I'm gonna go," I got up and exited the house.

As I was getting in my car I looked back to see Kich still watching me. This was beginning to feel too awkward. I was not about to have sex with Zay's best friend.

I rushed into my house and ran in my room. I was overtaken by a world wind of emotions. I had an urge to write Zay to see if he thought I should continue this and then I had a burning desire to run back to Kich. It was like something had been activated inside me and I couldn't escape it. I felt my breathing changing. It was like my lungs were closing up on me. I sat down and just breathed.

I have to write Zay. I have to at least get his advice and make sure it's ok with him that I'm working with Kich.

Bitch, Zay ass doesn't give a damn about you. He don't even text back when you hit him up. Wanna know what you owe Zay? Shit.

I knew I had a decision to make. So I did it anyways to prove my other-self wrong.

Zay

Hi.

The day passed and I still hadn't gotten a response.

Told yo' ass. Maybe you should text Kich and see what he is up to.

No, I'm not gonna text Kich after I just ran

136

out of his house.

I lied down and stared at the ceiling and then I got a text message. I checked to see who it was... it was Kich.

Kich

I apologize.
Can we start over?
I don't want to engage
in anything you don't.
I think I read your
signals wrong so that's
my fault.

It's ok. It's not your
fault.

Is that because I read
the signals correctly
or are you just trying
to not make me feel
bad?

I plead the 5th.
What are you up to?

Just finished recording
a song. It's gone be a
banga.

That's wassup.

Nude Picture Message
Oh my bad, wrong person.

Oh my gosh, his penis is perfect.

My mouth started to water at the sight of that picture and my vagina walls started to clench. I bit my lips as I kept looking. I wanted it in me.

I quickly came to my senses and deleted the picture.

Oh it's ok. I'll
just delete it
and pretend
I didn't see it.

Well you don't have
to do that.

Too late. I already
did.

I can send it again
if you want.

No, thank you.

How about this?
Video Message

I opened the message and it was Kich having sex with some woman. I couldn't stop watching. The way she was riding him and the way he bent her over and fucked her from the bottom. He smacked her ass and spreaded her cheeks. It was intriguing. I looked closer and I noticed that she was bound with some kind of rope.

Why did she have
rope on her?

Would you like me to
demonstrate for you?

I don't know if I'd
enjoy that. If I'm in
ropes how do I let you
know when something
hurts. I can't stop you
with my hands or resist.

That's kinda the point
lol.

I wouldn't like that.

There's also a certain thing
as a safe word.

A safe word?

Yes, that's what
you use if something
is getting out of hand
or is too much for
you. This isn't to harm
you. You would probably
enjoy it more than you
think.

And then it kicked in I was no longer

fighting my attraction. I was giving in. I was discussing this video as if it was optional for him to do it to me. I knew then I had to back out. I couldn't do that to Zay...right?

Probably not, well Kich I think I'm going to call it a night. It's been a long day and I'm exhausted.

I didn't sleep well that night. I kept tossing and turning while thinking about Kich. I knew now was a horrible time to talk to anyone because I was on the rebound. My heart was in shambles after my breakup with Zay and I knew it wasn't right to seek comfort from his best friend. I was going to have to tell Kich that we couldn't talk anymore in any form. I would just find someone else to record my audiobook with.

The next morning I woke up to a text message from Kich.

Kich Mawni

You should come over today.

Purpose?

Me...duh.

I need a better reason.

I'm just teasing
Vistoria, I'm having
a dinner party
and I'd like you
to come. So you
know that this is
just a business invite
please bring a friend.
Male or female.
Your choice.

> I may stop by then.
> Thanks for the invite.

Well you know
the address.
Dinner is served
at 7 but you are
welcome to come
at any time.

> Ok :)

I decided to invite Kara so she could get to
see the things I was telling her in person. She wore
a sexy black body suit and I wore a long black,
strap dress with slits on each side so my legs could
stick out. I loved how my legs looked in heels. I
had really toned legs with nice calf muscles.

Kich's house looked different around this
time. He had Hollywood lights flashing swaying
from side to side as we pulled up. He also had
Valet parking all the cars. I was impressed.

We walked in and it was a lot of people there. Some people wore masks.

"I didn't know this was a masquerade party," Kara said.

"Yea I didn't either. He didn't mention any special attire," I replied.

"I'm glad you could make it," I felt a cold chill on my back.

I turned around and it was Kich.

"I'm glad I came," I replied.

"And who's your friend?" he asked.

"This is Kara," I said.

"Hey, nice to meet you," Kara replied.

"The pleasure is mine," Kich slowly lifted Kara's hand and kissed it.

I saw Kara blushing.

Well maybe if Kara falls for him he'll stop coming after me.

And what will this solve? What will you win? Zay? A guy who never responds to you?

But it didn't matter to me I would be grateful if Kara took Kich off my hands. I even decided to give them more time to chat by saying I needed to go to the restroom.

"Hey Kich, which way is the bathroom? I'd like to get that out of the way before dinner and before I start drinking as well," I laughed.

"Choose. There's 3 down here and 3 upstairs. I do believe all the ones down here are occupied so please try upstairs 1st so you don't have to wait," Kich said.

"Ok. I'll be back Kara. Are you ok to stay here for a moment?" I asked.

"Oh sure, I'll find someone to mingle with while I wait," she replied.

"Excuse me," I pardoned myself from them.

I walked up the stairs and began to search for the bathroom. I wondered if Kich's bedroom was up here. It was so dark up there so I searched for a light in the hall. However, there was a light coming from somewhere. There was a red glow seeping from under one of the doors. I searched harder for a light because I wanted to see more. I finally stumbled across the hall light and turned it on. I immediately drew my attention back to this door that had the red light oozing around its perimeters. It looked like something off of Charmed. It was decorated with golden-brushed tree limbs and a very majestic looking doorknob. The knob was very ancient with a huge keyhole. I wondered if it was just a decorative door or if it really led to something. I had almost forgotten that my initial visit up there was to find the bathroom. I resumed my search for it just in case someone came upstairs. I found the bathroom to my right but something about this door was calling my name. I looked around to be sure I was still the only person up there and then I walked closer. I twisted the door slowly and pushed.

I could see some type of ceiling swings and bondage devices all over the room. There was a light that shined down on this beautiful circular bed that looked like it could hold at least 10 people comfortably. And on it was at least 5 people fucking each other in the most exotic way. From

143

what I could tell it was 3 girls and 2 guys. One of the guys was wearing a mask like what we had saw downstairs.

"Snooping are we?" Kich had followed me.

"What are you doing?" I snapped and closed the door.

"You almost scared me to death," I hit him.

"I can see that you are curious. You can go in if you want," he insisted.

"It's a really cool door so it caught my attention. I didn't know what was happening back there,"

I spun around and rushed downstairs.

"You don't have to be ashamed that you were intrigued Vistoria," Kich tried to convince me.

"I wasn't. I was lost and I opened the door by accident," I frantically looked for Kara.

He grabbed my hand very sternly and looked me in my eyes.

"Do not lie to me to my face Vistoria that's not very nice. Do you understand," he said.

"Yes I understand," I replied.

"Now were you intrigued?" he asked me again.

"Yes I was," I replied as if he had put me in some weird trance. All of a sudden my entire body just obeyed him.

"Was what?" he asked.

"I was intrigued," I said.

"Say 'Yes I was intrigued'," he demanded.

"Yes I was intrigued," I said like someone in a hypnosis.

"Now you may continue to search for your friend, but hurry you wouldn't want her curiosity to lead her upstairs," he laughed.

"Bastard," I said under my breath but then I kept moving because I didn't want him to come put his voodoo trance on me again.

I found Kara in the middle of two men as they both massaged her. One was massaging her back and the other was massaging and licking her feet. The one who was massaging her back had slightly taken her straps off her shoulder. He was getting closer and closer to her boobs.

"Yes, right there. You guys know how to turn a girl on," she said.

I couldn't let this go on. Kich was not about to invite us to his freak fest and turn me and my friend out.

"Kara come on, we're leaving," I interrupted.

"You're leaving. I'm enjoying myself, this massage is awesome and it's free," she replied.

"I'm ready to go Kara," I repeated.

"How are you going to invite me somewhere and then leave because you aren't having a good time? I want to stay. Besides dinner looks amazing and I'm starving," she demanded.

"Ok! Fine. We'll stay for dinner, but after that can we go?" I pleaded.

"Sure," she hopped up and we proceeded to the dining area.

Kich had the sleaziest servers I had ever seen. They wore aprons with nothing under it but a thong and some of them had their nipples poking out. I must say they had the prettiest, perkiest tits in the room though. Very lickable.

Did you just say that? Lesbo.

Surprisingly he had male servers as well. They didn't wear a shirt but at least had underwear on. The guest would fondle the servers all while eating. I never really thought about how pussy and pasta tasted together or penis and pudding. Nevertheless, it was something they all seemed to enjoy and they were very familiar with it.

Dinner was actually delicious and I was happy I stayed for that portion. Kara gave her number to her two mystery men. I can only imagine what'll happen if they ever meet up.

I escaped without seeing Kich again. A few days passed and I hadn't heard from him. I started to wonder if he was feeling some type of way. Although I should look at it as a good thing I was starting to feel uneasy. I didn't know if I wanted us to really break this thing or not. My emotions were so over the place with how I wanted to move forward with him.

Days passed and I still hadn't heard from Kich. I decided that when I did hear from him I was going to tell him how I wanted to break this off. I had enough time to myself to realize that I was ok. I didn't need to be introduced to his lifestyle. I could meet another guy in my city. A normal guy and that's what I was going to do.

I was on a date with a guy I had met while grocery shopping when Kich text me.

Kich Mawni

146

I'd like to see you.
What are you doing?

                              Is this about business?

Is it ever?

                                        Well then we
                                        have nothing
                                        to discuss.

What are you doing?

                                              I'm out.

Out doing what?

                                    I'm out on a date.

You didn't get
permission
to do that.

                                      I don't need it.

Feisty.

                                             Bite me.

I will, in time.

                                       I no longer want
                                       you to contact me.
                                       This isn't going to
                                                    work.

147

Sexually or
professionally?

Both. I'd prefer it if
you deleted my
number.

Noted.

I ended my date and I think he thought he
was coming in for the follow-up afterward. I exited
the car with a smile. I got in my room and lied on
the bed and I had an incoming message from Kich.

I'm near your
neighborhood. Kara
left a piece of jewelry
at my house. I
wanted to return it.
I will disappear
after this.

I was half sleep
at the moment
and just said yes.

Kich walked in my place looking around as
if he had left something there.
"The jewelry," I said.
"Oh yes, here you are," he replied.
"Thanks," I grabbed the necklace and sat it
on my dresser.

I looked around because I was waiting on Kich to leave.

"Nice place you have here," he said.

"Well aren't you the humble type," I replied.

"Have I done something to offend you Vistoria?" he asked.

My energy shifted because I realized I was in full attack mode.

"No you haven't," I responded.

"So why are you so mad at me? Is it because I'm merely shining light on a part of you that you didn't know you had or didn't care to admit," he said.

"I don't really want to discuss this now," I replied.

Kich stood up and walked closer to me. I looked him in his eyes and the connection busted.

Kich flipped me over on my knees and slid my shorts off then my panties. He spread my pussy lips and started to lick me from the back. He had his entire face in my ass and my pussy. He was taking long licks going back and forth between them both. Then he sat back on the bed and pulled me on top of him.

"Sit," he slid his cock into me and I started to ride him.

Are we really having sex without a condom right now? I'm going to regret this tomorrow.

"You're mine now," he said.

"Yes," I replied.

"Tell me," he pulled my hair.

"I'm yours now," I said as I continued to

bounce on top of him.

"Tell me how big of a slut you are," he put his hands around my neck.

"I'm such a slut," I repeated.

"Tell me how you let my friends all fuck you," he said.

Well that was only one friend Kich, but if this turns you on then sure.

"I'm such a slut and I fucked all your friends," I moaned.

"Yes you are. You're my slut," he continued as he grabbed my ass cheeks and thrusted up from the bottom.

He then threw me over and got on top of me. He stuck his cock back in me and started to choke me again.

"Such a good little whore aren't you," he said.

"Yes I am," I replied.

"Get on your knees," he said.

I got on my knees and he came all over my face.

Once he was finished he zipped up his pants and asked where my bathroom was. I pointed to the door. He walked in and came out with a towel. He threw it at me.

"Clean up," I wiped the cum off my face with the towel.

"Vistoria, I meant it when I said you were mine now. You might as well cancel all your dates. You won't be needing them. You're going to need all of your energy to keep up with me," he looked at me and then exited.

And that is how my love triangle started.

Chapter 6
<u>Peak</u>

I woke up the next morning and I just knew everything was a dream. There was no way that Kich and I had sex in that way last night. I dragged into the bathroom and looked in the mirror. My eyes bucked in horror. I had hickies and bite marks all over my chest and neck. My eye also had a slight red mark in it.

Was this from asphyxiation or having cum shots all over my face?

The strangest thing of them all was that this actually turned me on. I went to lie back down in my bed. I didn't know where I was headed in life. This definitely wasn't a normal relationship.

My phone vibrated and it was Kich. I wanted to bury my phone at the bottom of the ocean and continue with my normal life.

Kich Mawni

How did you sleep?

I decided that I didn't care to call him by his stage name anymore and just saved his number under his real name.

Kich

I slept pretty well.

I was very pleased
yesterday, I want
more of you.

Well that can be arranged.

153

Wait, what the fuck? No it can't.
Oh shut up, yes it can. Punk.

I got tired of the constant debate going on in my head.

Come now.

Why did everything seem like an order? Don't I get asked if I want to do something or not?

Everything about him had an effect on me that scared me but drew me in even more. And not like a "scared he'll harm me" way. It was mostly a fear from the unfamiliar, but if what he had to offer was anything like last night then it was going to be amazing. There was something inquisitively pulling me in deeper and deeper.

I walked in Kich's house and called his name.

"Kich," I said.

"I'm in here," he replied.

I continued to walk and look around because with a house that big "in here" could still be a number of places. I just hoped he was anywhere but the room of doom upstairs.

"Which room are you in?" I asked then I saw his hand poke out of one. I walked in and it was his studio. It was very nice.

"What are you recording?" I asked.

"Us," he smiled.

"Us, and exactly what are you recording of us?" I asked nervously.

"Not visuals, unless you want to. But I want to record the sounds of me fucking you," he

154

replied.

"Oh, sounds interesting. When do we start?" I asked.

"Now," he pulled me down on top of him and started to kiss on me.

He bit my lip and then continued to move up my face. It's like he had a rotation of kissing, licking, and biting. And then he bit my cheek really hard, so hard that I gasped out in pain. Then he came right behind it and gave it the softest kiss that made it all better.

"Suck it," he started to unzip his pants and pulled his cock out.

I deep-throated it and held it in my mouth for almost a minute while licking his balls.

He pulled my head up and then slapped me.

"Spit on it," he said.

"Ok," I replied.

He pulled my head back up.

"Say yes," he looked me in my eyes.

"Yes," I said.

"Yes what," he replied.

"Yes sir," I said.

"Good girl," he shoved his cock back in my mouth.

He then grabbed my head and started thrusting his cock in my mouth really fast and really hard. My mouth was regurgitating so much spit it was if it was climaxing. I never knew that my throat could take so much impact at once. And then the weirdest thing of all my sexual encounters happened.

"Uhhh, Uhhh, oh my gosh...I'm cumming,"

the words leaped from my mouth.

Hold on, what? What the entire fuck? Am I having an orgasm from giving him head? This is not possible.

My body wouldn't stop shaking as my mouth was still wrapped around his cock.

"Good girl," he rubbed my head and then let his load off in my mouth.

I swallowed it.

"I'm impressed," then he kissed me in my mouth.

I sat there on the floor trying to compose what just happened.

He turned around and hit stop on his recording equipment.

"That'll make for some fun background noises in my next sex song," he laughed.

"I'm sure it will. Don't I get paid for that," I joked.

He looked at me with a very stern eye. It was so stern that it made me uncomfortable. I didn't know if I had said something wrong.

"Vistoria come here," he motioned for me to come closer.

He looked at me and said, "You can have whatever you want from me."

"I was just joking. I don't really want anything," I said.

"Never tell a man you don't want anything because if he takes it to heart when you want something later you can't get mad because it was your command," he said.

"Ok," I said.

"We men always want something so it's not a crime for you to want something as a woman," he continued.

"Speaking of which, take your bottoms off and bend over. I want to fuck that sweet, little pussy while your orgasms is still hot and oozing out," he demanded.

I took my pants and my underwear off and I bent over with my hands on the chair.

"Hands on the desk bad girl," he said.

"I am a bad girl," I replied.

Hey I responded that time without being told. I think I'm starting to get the hang of this.

He slid into me and I just remembered every reason why condoms should not be allowed during sex. I could feel every inch of him inside me. I could feel the curved head as it penetrated my opening and gave its nozzle a resting place inside me. I could feel his veins pulsing inside of me and his shaft stretching me. I was so relaxed and I just let him have his way with my body. I moved away from the desk and touched my toes. He continued going in and out of my pussy. He started to smack my ass harder and harder. Spreading my cheeks as he filled my pussy with his thick cock.

He snatched me by my hair and leaned me against his chest.

"You're a filthy little cunt you know that," he said.

"Yes I'm a nasty little fuck toy," I replied.

"Bend back over, I'm not done fucking

you," he bent me over and continued pounding my pussy.

I realized I was starting to gain my confidence in our relationship. I was starting to be more expressive.

"Yes, Kich. Spit in my mouth baby," I bellowed out as he fucked me in missionary.

He choked me harder and spit in my mouth then slapped me. It felt so amazing. I loved the feeling of being owned by him.

After we were done we lied on the floor just looking at each other.

"So do we shower now," I asked.

"You know you talk a lot for a sub," he said.

"For a what?" I asked.

He sighed.

"Come on, let's go shower," he stood up and grabbed my hand.

I followed him up the hallway and then up the stairs. He was walking towards the room of doom.

"Isn't there showers in some of the other rooms?" I asked.

"Yes, but I want to shower in this one," he said.

I just shut up and continued to follow him. He twisted the knob to the room and we walked inside.

"So what do you call this room?" I asked.

"I call it the Power Room," he said.

"Why would you call it that? I wouldn't feel very powerful if I was chained up in all of these contraptions," I said as I looked around at his displays.

"See that's where you are wrong, you have more power as a sub than you know. I'm not me without you," he said.

"Oh how sweet," I remarked.

"No, it's true. A good sub brings out the best part of a true Dom. You are what makes me powerful. I am powerful because you have given me yours," he continued.

Oh gosh, he is really getting deep with this talk. I can see this means a lot to him.

"Believe it or not but it takes a strong woman to relinquish all her power to a man and be a submissive," he looked at me and rubbed his fingers through my hair.

"There is nothing weak about that, don't ever forget it," he kissed me.

I don't know, but I did feel powerful after that statement. And I sure didn't feel weak when we were having sex. It was the most thrilling sex I had ever had. I finally understood how pain could be pleasure.

We made it to the bathroom located in the Power Room. It was really nice. The shower was walk-in with a glass closure in one section and then there was a very large Jacuzzi

, Jetted tub. He had a flat screen mounted on the wall. And then I noticed random holes in the walls of the bathroom.

"Why are there holes in the walls?" I asked.

"What do you mean?" he asked.

Then I pointed to the one that was next to me.

"Oh I keep forgetting you're a newbie. It's a glory hole babe," he laughed.

"And that was supposed to explain to me what it is," I responded.

"How about I just show you," then he exited the bathroom.

I looked around trying to figure out how he was going to show me from outside the bathroom. And then I felt something poking me on my leg and I jumped.

"What the hell Kich," then I looked down and saw his penis poking through the hall in the wall.

"Do you see now?" he was speaking through the wall.

"You could give me head or I could fuck you. And for those who really wanna have some fun you could switch partners and let everyone in the house take turns fucking you," then he walked back in.

"But we're not there yet. I'm definitely not in the mood to share you with another man. Maybe a woman, would you like that?" he touched my lip.

"Yes sir," I licked his finger.

"That's my girl. We'll have to make that happen," he walked me over to the shower.

"Shower or tub?" he looked at me.

"Whichever you choose is fine," I said.

"I was going to take a shower but I feel like relaxing so the tub it is," he said.

He turned the water on and it started to jet out. When we got in it felt so good just relaxing on him. I felt like I never wanted to leave this place. We were engulfed in bubbles and I was in paradise.

"I love being with you Vistoria, you bring something out of me that I haven't felt in a while," he said.

"You're genuine and that's something that's hard to find these days. I respect you for that," he continued.

"I feel the same way about you Kich. You have shown me a new way of life and I was scared at first. Now I'm intrigued and grateful to have you as my teacher," I said.

"I'm merely bringing out of you what was already in you. We often bury those things that are apart of human nature. Society has taught us that everything we desire is wrong, but guess what we are just like animals. We get aroused and nature created outlets for us to work off these arousals. It was humans who created laws to contain our desires by," he responded.

Kich always made really good points. I did feel free with him. I felt like all my fantasies could come to life with him.

He started to nibble on my neck. We sat in the tub until the bubbles had disappeared.

Once we got out the tub we went to his bedroom and went to sleep.

These moments started to become regular.

Kich was my Dom now and it wasn't anything I wouldn't do for him. We weren't in a relationship but more like an agreement. There were moments where I was summoned just to give him head and sent back on my way. This might sound demeaning but for me it was intriguing. I enjoyed every bit of it. I never knew what to expect from Kich. It seemed like just when I thought sex was getting familiar with Kich he would throw in a twist.

This particular night I was summoned and told to wear nothing but a black robe and heels.

I walked into the house and made my way to the Power Room.

Kich didn't take any time stripping me and cuffing me to the bed. He put his cock in my mouth and I started to suck him. Kich then turned around and put his ass in my face.

Am I supposed to lick it?

I had heard of "tossing the salad" but I had never done it before. If this turned him on then I figured it was no time like the present to start. I just moved my tongue around and hoped I was doing it right. I figured I was when he un-cuffed me and commanded me to massage his balls with my hands while licking his ass.

Does this mean Kich is bisexual or do straight men like their ass licked?

I had many questions on this topic but I wasn't going to ask at the moment.

Kich came in that position so I knew it was something he enjoyed.

Once we finished in the Power Room we

showered and went to sleep in Kich's bedroom. This seemed to be a routine. We never slept in the Power Room probably because it was covered in cum by the time we finished.

Before we went to sleep Kich gave me an amazing foot massage. I loved Kich's massages because they always included his tongue.

"Get my foot out of your mouth Kich," I joked.

"Nope, I love how you taste. Every part of you," he kept sucking on my feet.

"You're so nasty," I said and turned my nose up at him.

"Do you own a passport?" he asked.

Kich was always so spontaneous. That night he booked us both tickets to Marseilles, France. He said he just wanted to get away for a while and that he loved the caves and sailing on the oceans there.

Our seats were right next to each other in first class. I must've taken 1000 selfies. I took selfies of us eating, sleeping, drinking wine. These moments were beautiful and it was strange that I was spending them with Zay's best friend.

Wow, this is the 1st time I've mentioned Zay in a long time.

The lines began to be more blurred and blurred. It wasn't as if he was Zay's best friend anymore, but it was as if he was just my Kich. My beast with a troubled past and I was Belle. And I was his belle, the most beautiful of them all.

We got to our place and it was amazing. He had gotten an apartment for the week. Although I probably wouldn't be doing much cooking it was still an awesome gesture.

The first day we just went out to sight see. I had been out of the country before, but never to France. It was always a dream of mine to travel there. I think I smiled as we entered into every door to look around.

"You seem extremely happy," Kich said.

"I am. I'm so happy I'm surprised I haven't exploded into little pieces," I laughed.

"Why are you so happy?" he asked.

"I love French culture so it's an honor to even be here," I said.

"OMG, macaroons. Real macaroons, I've always wanted to try one," I leaped.

"Well get one, get two or however many you want," he said.

I got a ton of macaroons in the prettiest box with a bow.

"Another thing on my to-do list would be to get a baguette, Brie, and some wine. I don't know if that's the exact order I'm supposed to get them in but I'm dying to try some authenticity," I squealed.

"When I decided to come here I had no idea that you would love it so much. I'm also happy that I chose this place," he said.

"This brie is delicious. Like who knew that cheese could taste so good," I said.

"Can I have a bite?" Kich asked.

"No, you can't. All mine," I joked and then I fed him a piece.

"Aren't you wearing a dress?" he asked.

"Yes, why?" I responded.

"Come," he grabbed my hand.

I was wearing a tri-color, strapped dress that hung to the ground and blew ferociously as I walked. The main color was a sky blue and it had mixes of yellow, pink, green, and orange dashed in it. My boobs sat in the cuffs amazingly and I didn't have to wear a bra. I was happy about that as well.

I had grabbed a small rolling basket from one of the side shops earlier because grocery bags charged at most of the stores and I had done tons of shopping. I figured it was better to pay for one thing to store all my purchases than hauling around tons of bags.

Kich was leading me somewhere and I had no idea.

Then he paused and took his cock out of the zipper hole.

"What are you doing? We're outside," I said smiling.

"What does it look like?" he asked.

"Come," then he pulled me backwards. My dress was very flowy and long so when I was backed up on him it almost looked as if we were just a couple leaned on one another. He lifted my dress in the back and stuck it in me.

I moaned out in the alley when he entered me. I could see people walking by but none of them seemed to be paying us much attention. Kich continued going and gripping my waist really close making me take all of his cock.

"Oh you're such a dirty whore. Look at you getting fucked outside," he whispered in my ear

165

and then bit me.

We ended up getting two viewers. A couple was passing by and they stopped to watch.

"Wank me baby," the guy said to his girlfriend. She put her hands in his pants and started to jack him off. I assumed it was the term used in this area to describe jerking off as we Americans say. It was the most exhilarating thing I had ever done in my life and the audience made it so much better. I caught eye contact with the girl a few times while I was getting pounded and she was on her knees wanking and sucking him off.

Kich came in me and I felt his creamy load oozing out of my pussy and sopping down my leg. I then pulled up my underwear to catch the remaining drippings and Kich released my dress from his hands. Then Kich zipped his pants back up and we walked out of the alley as if nothing had happened.

"So where are we off to now?" I asked.

"I think we've had enough adventure for one day. What do you say we go back to the apartment and drink this wine I got you?" he suggested.

"Sounds like a plan to me," and we headed back towards our living area.

"I am sure I'll never forget my stay in Marseilles now," I kissed Kich's hands.

"Can we shower now?" I asked.

"What you don't like walking around with my cum inside you?" he laughed.

"Well it's not that," I replied.

"You may shower, I have some things I

need to finish going over," he said.

"Ok, be back in a bit," I hopped off the bed and headed towards the bathroom.

Kich had brought me some body washes while we were out shopping. I lathered up with my loofa and enjoyed my scenery. I couldn't believe that I was in one of my favorite places in the world with such an exciting man. I was surprised Kich didn't join me. I got out and walked back in the room where he was.

"What have you been in here doing," I snuggled up under him.

"I booked us a boat for tomorrow to view the Calanques," he said.

"So that's what you were out here doing. I can't wait," before I knew it I was dozing off into dreamland.

We got up early the next morning to catch our boat at the docking area. I wore a cream-colored floppy sun hat with a bright yellow two-piece bathing suit and a see-through yellow cover up that hung down to my knees. Kich only wore shorts and his Nike slides. He stuffed a shirt in my bag along with a jacket. He said that it got windy in certain areas and told me I might would need it.

I loved watching the waves of the Mediterranean smash into the side of the boat. The boat was really nice. It had a nice seating area underneath and it had a kitchen where they prepared the most delicious food. Once we arrived at a good stopping point the bow of the boat opened and formed a small pool. It opened right up into the ocean and a lot of people swam there.

Some people climbed down and swam in the open waters.

"Do you wanna go swimming?" I asked.

"Yes we can. How much of a dare devil are you?" he had this look on his face so I was almost scared to answer.

"I'm here with you, obviously I'm very daring," I laughed.

"Well let's swim over to those cliffs and dive," he said with much excitement.

"Cliff diving? Well I've never tried it but there's a first time for everything. Let's do it," I said.

I took my cover up off and climbed down the side of the boat.

We had to swim a short distance to make it to the cliffs. Some of our fellow boat riders had already beat us to it. Once we started climbing the cliff I knew we hadn't thought this all the way through.

"I'm sure some tennis shoes would've made this so much easier," I scoffed.

"You're almost there keep going and stop complaining," he hit me on my butt.

"I'm not complaining but you're not gonna want me when I have scaly alligator feet from climbing these rocks and rough man hands," I said.

"While you're complaining you failed to realize that you made it," he said.

I looked around and we were at the top of the cliff. Well at lease half way. If we climbed to the top Kich probably would've thrown me back down by now. The Calanques were beautiful and to look out into the ocean from this view was even more amazing.

"Ok, so you know the way back down right?" Kich asked interrupting my admiration.

"Oh yea that's right, we aren't climbing back down," I looked down and braced myself.

"I can do this," I looked at him.

"I can do this," then I took a deep breath.

"Do you want me to go first?" he asked.

"Then I'll be up here all by myself," I said.

"I mean you can always climb back down and turn into a lizard or whatever you talked about or you can evolve into a mermaid. What will it be?" he looked at me waiting for an answer.

"You're right, I'm a mermaid," and then I dove into the water.

The drop seemed like it took forever. I could feel nothing but space and air around me.

I felt as if I went to the bottom of the ocean with how much impact my body had hitting the water. I finally saw sunlight and then I poked my head out. I survived. I looked up on the cliff at Kich and smiled. He may couldn't see it from there, but I was extremely happy. I felt like one person jumped from the cliff and I felt like another person rose from the water. I hadn't felt so free in my life. Kich's dare devil side was bringing a person out of me that I was afraid of at first, but I slowly started to embrace. She was beautiful. She was fearless. She lived a life without rules. She was me.

I realized that Kich was about to jump and I had better swam closer to the boat so he wouldn't smash me. I got a good distance away and looked up at him jumping. He was such a showoff and had to do a trick with his. I'm sure he had done this before that's why he was so adamant about getting me to go. He loved to freak me out.

He swam closer to me and when he got in my reach I swam up to him and kissed him. We stayed there for a moment just twirling in the water and enjoying the waves.

When we got back to the boat we both wrapped up in our towels and went to grab some lunch. I had duck and some kind of pasta that was really amazing. Kich had a medium-rare burger. I wasn't up to try my burgers like that just yet. Which was probably bias on my part because I'd eat a steak in that form.

After we finished eating we went to the lower deck and relaxed. The temperature on the ocean had started to drop and a full stomach always made me sleepy. I coiled tightly under Kich and went to sleep. I was awakened by Kich telling me we had arrived back to the dock and that it was time to get off the boat.

We went back to our apartment and fell asleep. The next day I picked something for us to do. I wanted to go to the Notre-Dame de la Garde aka Our Lady of the Guard or what some of the natives referred to as the Lady of Marseilles. There was so much beauty in that basilica.

"Ok, I see you have some taste. This was a good spot," Kich teased me.

"See I told you to trust me," I replied.

"Wow, we can see the entire city from

here," I looked over at Kich who was snapping photos.

It was at that moment that it happened. It was that moment that I relived the intensity of jumping off that cliff yesterday. I was falling, hard. Kich's connection with me was almost deeper than anything I had ever felt. He got me, every part of me. Kich understood the parts of me that people would say were weird and call me names for. Kich took me as I was and didn't try to change me. What we had was deeper than surface level, it touched my soul.

Five Questions
What is a soul mate?
Does one have the power to break it?
In time, does it fade?
Can you tell your heart to stop loving the other?
Will it listen?

Chapter 7
<u>Reality</u>

Our last few days were spent just enjoying each other's company and going down to the beach. A part of me would always be in Marseilles.

I don't know why in my life extreme highs seemed to always be followed by extreme lows. I just knew that Kich and I would be inseparable after this. But maybe men put "love" in a different folder than women do. Maybe that's it. Maybe they don't store love at all. Maybe love goes straight to the shredder.

On the flight back over to the States Kich seemed like he had something on his mind. He was very quiet with me. I would play around and he wouldn't laugh much. I could feel an energy change and I didn't know why. It was so strong that it almost made me sick to my stomach and I wanted to throw up. I couldn't wait for the plane to land so I could get off and go to my house. Maybe he felt smothered by me and just needed his space. Whatever the reason I didn't think it was fair to me. I thought it was very inconsiderate to take me on a trip and make me feel the way he did only to leave paradise and start mistreating me.

"Have I done something to you?" I asked.

"No, I just wasted a lot of time in France and now I have some catching up to do," he remarked.

"Wasting time? So now I'm a waste of time?" I asked.

"Vistoria, I don't have time for you to be getting in your feelings and rewording my statement," he snapped.

I lowered my head and looked out the window. My heart was still longing for the Kich with the moments I had just shared. I didn't want to believe that all that was just an act. I wanted to believe that everything I had experienced was real and that it wasn't just to get his fix for a week.

Maybe he does this all the time and I was just a pawn in his game.

We landed and got our luggage.

"Are we taking the same car or what?" I asked.

"No, I called Rico to take you home and Melanie is bringing my car," Kich said.

"Oh, Melanie. Great," I snarked.

Rico was Kich's personal shopper/driver/anything else Kich needed in an errand form. Melanie was something like a nanny when it came to errands, but she also was Kich's sub. We all had a threesome one night. She's pretty good with her tongue.

Melanie swerved in driving the BMW and it was the 1st time I wanted to drag her ass out of the car. She got out in some shorts that were way up her ass and a bralette. The bitch never wore any real clothes. She grabbed Kich's bags and placed them on the backseat.

"Welcome home Daddy," she kissed him on his cheek.

"Welcome home Misses," she kissed me on my cheek.

"I'll get at you later," he kissed me on the forehead and put my suitcase in the car that Rico was driving.

"Fine," I hopped in the car and slammed the door.

Tears started to roll down my cheek but I quickly wiped them away. I wasn't going to shed tears over a jackass. Even if I was thinking the jackass could possibly be my other half in this twisted world.

A few days passed and I hadn't heard anything from Kich. I felt like he was now doing the same thing Zay had done but it was even stranger because we just had such a perfect week together. As always I started to retrace my steps to see if it was anything I had done. I know I was a little attitudinal when I got out the car, but it was only because he was being so rude to me. That couldn't be why he was now ignoring me. I did come on my period the next day so maybe I was more irritated when he was giving me the silent treatment than normal.

Yes, this was classic me. I always found a reason to blame myself when any guy I dated started to act up. I knew I had a slight temper so at times I felt I ran them off. Was I supposed to just shut up and let him have his moment in the car or was I supposed to address it?

More days passed and he was still very quiet. I was off my period by now so my hormones were raging. I decided to text him to see what he was doing. One part of the agreement we had was that I was only to have sex with him. I couldn't keep that up if he wasn't even talking to me.

Kich

What are you doing?

I waited for some hours and I hadn't gotten a response.

Hello? Why are you being an ass this week?

I waited a little longer and I still hadn't received a reply.

Why aren't you texting me back?

Look quit texting me like I'm your man. Damn.

Are you serious right now? You're crazy. I was only texting you because I was horny. But oh well guess I'll hit someone else up.

I couldn't believe how he was acting and it was so abrupt. I realized I couldn't keep putting energy into trying to figure out what sparked Kich's new attitude towards me.

Quit texting me like I'm your man. Rang through my head daily.

Bastard.

So I let some time pass and I continued life as if there was no Kich. I even hooked up with an ex of mine to pass the time. Before I was trying to save my body for him. I didn't want to have sex with anyone else because there was no point. He was fulfilling every sexual desire I had ever had, until now. To make matters worse that week I was extremely horny. I'm talking about the type of horny that leaves you hot flashes while you're out in public grocery shopping. The kind of horny that you have to masturbate at random times just to keep yourself sane. I'm talking about the kind of horny that you want to fuck the mailman just because he has testosterone and a penis.

My ex was good enough to hold me over. We fucked in the back of his truck for a quick thrill. His sex had always been good but damn it wasn't Kich's. I kept wanting to be choked and have him cum all over me and in me to show he owned me. I wanted him to give me commands and call me names. We fucked with a condom and he came within 10 minutes. The best thing about his sex was that his dick was really big and it hit all the good spots inside me.

The next day I was sitting with Kara watching movies and having our girl's night. It was good to be busy and having fun but every quiet moment, I thought of Kich. It's like he now owned my thoughts.

What kind of Dom just lets his Sub do whatever she wants? Why hasn't he come over here and threw me into a wall and made me suck him?

It was becoming hard to smile and laugh at the movie all while balancing all of these thoughts

177

about Kich.

"Are you good?" Kara asked.

"Yes, I'm fine. My thoughts are just running rampant right now," I said.

"I'm gonna get more wine, do you want another glass?" I asked Kara.

"Pour me up," she smiled back with her glass in the air.

So the night started to wind down and we both fell asleep in Kara's bed. I was later awakened by a text message.

Kich

Nights like this
I hate you ditched me.

No you don't.

I was going to try to milk this thing because now he had lost. He made the first contact in the war.

Yes I do, I'm staring at
one of your videos now.

Wow, he keeps my videos?

I was turned on and scared at the same time.

Wait, he's mad at me. I hope he doesn't leak it on social media. Well that wouldn't be good for his image so I should be safe. Hopefully.

I mean you were rude
to me for no reason like
I was hounding you so
I backed off. You
made me feel
horrible.

I didn't know that
was rude.

I just felt it was uncalled
for and you say things
a lot being inconsiderate.
I know we haven't made
anything official but
how you said it was rude.
Especially how we just spent
an entire week together
on an amazing trip.
I just felt like I earned
a little more respect than
that. I know you're not
my man and you're not
big on the relationship thing.
You thought I was tripping
from a girlfriend standpoint.
I was tripping because
I wanted to have sex
and you weren't cooperating.
That's what we have an
arrangement on.
How many times have
I been busy or working

179

and answered a call for
you because you wanted
to hear me moan on the phone?
How many times have
I drove to your house
just to give you head
and leave simply
because you asked.
I do freaky shit to you
I have never done in my
entire life and you trip
on me about some freaking
text messages? I never once
threw it in your face what
we were when you ask for
crazy shit but you did that
to me and I didn't like it.

Understood.

*What the hell? Did he just text me one word
when I just wrote him a book?*

Leave me alone.

I'm about to cum
watching your video.
That pussy is so perfect.

Do whatever you want.

This was the first time that his sexual
proposals weren't appealing to me. I didn't like this

because I had become emotional over him. My hurt was screaming louder than my hormones.

You're being a bad girl,
Daddy's going to have to
put you back in your place.

I wanted to scream. How dare he try to control me and I am pissed off right now.

There's no point in this
arrangement anymore.

And then he sent a picture of his penis.
Picture Message
He is the reason.
You know what happens
whenever he's inside you.

And just like a fish, I was hooked again. We set up a date to meet the next day. That morning I text him to see where he wanted to meet. I never knew if it was going to be his house, a grocery store, on side of the road, in an alley... I figured he'd want to be somewhere private because he was going to "put me back in my place."

Kich

Wake up at 6AM.

Ok.

With Kich I knew it was a purpose if he was telling me that so I made sure to set me an alarm.

I woke up at 6AM and laid in the bed for a

moment then I text Kich.

Kich

Where are we meeting at?

Knock, Knock.

Huh?

Then there was a knock on the door.
*Oh no, are we meeting here. He doesn't
give me any kind of warnings.*

I grabbed my robe, as if it mattered and
walked to the door.

I opened the door and it was his driver,
Rico.

"Oh hey, Rico," I said.

"What are you doing here?" I continued.

"I had orders to give you this room key and
to pick you up Miss Jefferson," he said.

"Oh ok, I'll be there in a second, just let
me..." he cut me off.

"Miss Jefferson, I was told to get you right
away and to not let you do anything else," he
interrupted.

"Hold on Rico," I said as I started to text
Kich.

Kich

I can't even shower
or comb my hair?
Can I brush my
teeth?

I didn't get a reply.

182

"Miss Jefferson, we need to go now," Rico pleaded.

I scooped up my shoes in my hands and my jacket and scurried out the door. I was still sleepy since it was so early. I immediately fell back asleep once I got in the car. I woke up in between and chatted with Rico then fell back asleep. I was awaken by Rico lightly poking me.

"Miss Jefferson, we are here," he said.

I walked in the hotel room that must've had some type of light prevention shades because it was dark although the sun was bright today. I called out his name as I walked in. I felt like I was in a scary movie and being led to my doom. No lights were visible except this one burning candle in the corner. And then he came from the shadows and choked me on the wall while kissing me passionately. I had on my robe and sneakers. He quickly got his fingers inside of me. I propped my leg up on a nearby dresser so he could really get a good grip on me. I could tell he liked how wet I was because I could feel his package starting to rise. He took his hands out my pants and put them in my mouth. I licked all my juices off of his fingers. Then he slapped me.

"You know you're in trouble right?" he asked.

"Yes," I said softly.

"Yes what?" he growled.

"Yes sir," I replied.

"On your knees," he demanded.

I got on my knees and he shoved his cock

in my mouth. I began to suck on his head and work my way down. I deep-throated him and I could feel his body tense up. I wrapped one hand around his shaft and started massaging his penis as I sucked him. I licked his balls and then buried my face in his ass. He always melted when I did that. He choked me again and smashed my face with his balls and ass. I just kept my tongue out and continued licking. This once seemed weird to me but now it was intriguing to me to see him become my bitch.

He started to call my name, " Vistoria! You're so good. Why are you so freaky? Damn."

I could tell I was driving him crazy.

Kich once told me that the sub had more power than they thought... This was one of the times were I could see that being right. He was completely under my spell. He pulled me up and swung me on to the bed. Then he climbed on top of me and entered my pussy. He then started to switch between my mouth and my pussy. Then back and forth. The final time I sucked him, I could tell he was about to explode. I stayed on his balls a few seconds later just because I wanted the cum to be practically seeping out when I got ready to catch it. I came up and it was erupting. I took it all in my mouth and licked off all the cum that had dripped somewhere else. I looked up and he was sleep. I thought maybe he was pretending but 5 minutes later he still hadn't moved.

Did I kill him? I've seen those people on TV go to the hospital after certain orgasms.

I could hear him breathing so I didn't panic

long. He woke up and looked from side to side.

"How long was I sleep?" he asked.

"For a while," I said.

I grabbed one of the alcohol beverages that were in the mini fridge.

Kich got up and pulled his pants back on and turned on a light.

I looked over at him and he looked stressed out.

"So what's been going on? You've been very strange lately," I said and took a sip of my drink.

He was just quiet.

"Ok, this silent treatment has got to stop. You're starting to freak me out," then I started laughing.

I looked up and I could see Kich's jawline bulging out.

"Vistoria, everything isn't a fucking game," he got up and threw his chair across the room.

"Ok, I think I officially know what it means when they say you can wake up on the wrong side of the bed. You're tripping. Hard," I said and rolled my eyes.

"When's the last time you talked to Zay," he grunted.

"Zay? I haven't..." and then he cut me off.

"Bitch, don't lie to me," he yelled.

"I don't know what you're talking about. I haven't talked to Zay. I haven't talked to Zay since before we got serious," I forced out choking back tears.

I walked up to him and tried to touch his

hand.

"Why are you acting like this?" I reached out for him but he snatched away.

"You're a liar," he finished grabbing his clothes.

"Lying about what? I don't know what you're talking about Kich," I walked towards him again.

"Stay the fuck away from me," he snatched away again.

He headed for the door and I ran and got in front of it.

"Are you going to leave me? Where are you going?" I pleaded.

He grabbed me by my neck and spoke very firm in my ear.

"I'm only going to tell you one more time. Get your ass from in front of the door before I break both of you," he threatened.

I looked down as tears filled my eyes and I stepped from in front of the door. I wiped my tears and cried for hours. I didn't even pay attention to what hotel I was at. Rico had picked me up so I had no way of leaving. I knew I was going to have to get in touch with Kara somehow. I sat there replaying what I did wrong this time. I kept coming up short. Then I noticed the transition.

He kept mentioning Zay.

The truth still remained I hadn't talked to Zay, but why would Kich think I had. I hadn't even checked up on Zay via social media. It was hard to on most sites because he blocked me after the last break up. Kara was still friends with him so I thought I'd log into her page and check.

Yes, I have my bestie's password. Don't you?

I logged onto her Instagram and went to his page. He had a group photo up with some guys. I knew a few of them from the network marketing business and early college years.

I don't see it. What's the big deal? Why is Kich tripping?

I checked the date and it was 2 days ago. Then it hit me. These guys lived in Memphis. I felt myself having a panic attack.

Oh fuck, oh fuck. No, no, no. No, Zay is not back. Please no. Oh God. He's gonna hate me. He's gonna hate me.

I couldn't even make it to the trash or the garbage I vomited right there on the floor.

Fuck, what am I gonna do? What am I gonna do. Kich must think I want Zay back. Do I? Oh God. Why did I talk to them both? I should've just stuck it out with Zay right? But I partially feel that me and Kich are meant to be.

I just screamed out at the top of my lungs. I had to get out of that room. I had to get out of that town.

I know I'll move to a new city away from them both. I won't even announce it. I'll start looking today. That's what I'll do.

I grabbed my phone and called Kara.
"Hello."
"Bitch, where are you?"
"Leaving the mall, what's up."
"I got myself in a world of trouble. I need you to

come get me."

"Where are you?"

"I don't even know but I'll send my location to you. Hopefully, it's not too far."

"Bitch, how do you not know where the fuck you are? Were you kidnapped?"

"Kind of, by Kich. He left me. He's mad at me."

"That ugly bastard."

"Zay is back."

"Aww hell, here you go. You better choose wisely."

"Choose. It's not a choice I can make. They're both amazing in so many ways and they're both shit in so many ways. I just want to like somebody normal. I'm looking for a new place to live when I get home. I'm going to start looking at jobs in other cities. The network marketing can hold me off for a while. The numbers have started dropping so I can't solely depend on that right now."

"Yea I know. I've been thinking the same thing too. I think we have spread our wings enough here. Let's do it."

"Well I'll send you my location and once we get home we can start looking at new places some where else."

"Cool, I'm on my way once I get it."

Kara was my down bitch. She was always up for the cause. That was one thing about us. We lived the life of wanderers so we drifted everywhere. Neither of us had children to look after so when we felt like it we just picked up and left. No explanations. No warnings.

Kara Poo <3

Damn, bitch.
You're an hour
away. How tf
didn't you
realize you were
riding for an hour.

I slept part of the
way and talked the
other part. It was
early when Rico
picked me up.

I can't believe
Kich. He's a fucking
asshole. I hate
him now.

Join the party.

I sat on the bed and looked around the
room in disbelief. My life seemed perfect some
weeks ago and now it had started to spiral out of
control.

I finally got in the car with Kara and we
discussed our plans.

"What about Atlanta, it's pretty popping
and it'll be a good move for our careers," Kara
said.

"Yea I was thinking that too and it's still a
city so it'll be plenty to do," I agreed.

"Atlanta it is," we said and high-fived.
"New beginnings, I'm ready," I said.

Chapter 8
<u>Prey</u>

We both went home and started to look for things to do while we were there. The cost of living was higher so we knew we would want to add some extra income. We had been warned that you didn't want to live in certain areas because it was big on robberies.

It didn't take long for us to hear back from jobs that already wanted to hire us. I was going to be working as an editor for a company. I could make my own hours so I liked that it still left room for my freedom and random outings. I hit my cousin Cookie up to see if we could crash with her while we looked for a place there. She had plenty of room and a dope place so it was perfect. When I was younger I looked up to Cookie. She had a way with men that I admired. They all groveled over her and she undoubtedly owned this energy and was not ashamed. Cookie owned her sexuality and what Cookie wanted, Cookie got...including your man or your husband. Cookie's logic was simple.

"No one can control you but you. If you wanna do some shit then do it. Fuck people and they feelings," she said once I told her about my love triangle. It really was her response to anything in life.

I loved being around Cookie and Kara. Girl's night out started to get better and better. Cookie had the hookup on all the clubs and she always paid for everything. Cookie was a boss. She had her own clothing boutique and a makeup line. Plus, some of her eligible Bachelor's and non-Bachelor's dropped off plenty cake to her.

"Y'all know I got space here so I don't

know why y'all keep looking for a spot. I mean hell y'all got y'all own room," Cookie said.

"I mean true, but you know we said before we came it was temporary so we didn't want to wear out our welcome," I said.

"Exactly," Kara pitched in.

"Well all I'm saying is stack ya bread, stay as long as you like. Hell I like having somebody around other than these niggas," she laughed.

"I appreciate that. Thank you," I responded.

We were all sitting around eating our oxtails; it was one of Cookie's favorite things to order. I heard my phone go off and I looked down and saw it was Kich.

Oh gosh, here we go.

I had been gone for almost a month and a half now and I hadn't said anything to Kich. Zay taught me well on how to do the whole "pick up and leave without warning."

Kich

Vistoria.

What?

I'm sorry.

Oh you know how
to apologize now.
Charming.

I was wrong for
leaving you that
day. I needed to

193

get some fresh
air to control
my emotions.
I came back
and you were
gone.

Why didn't you say
something that day?
I cried until I made
myself sick. You left
me without any
transportation.
Kich your abuse
has just added up
and I can't take it
anymore. You are
toxic to me and it's
about time I stop
living this lie as
if you are going
to be anything
more to me than
you are right now.

Can I please just
come see you. I
need to see you.

I don't want to see
you. Ever again in
my life. You disgust
me.

I didn't quite feel this exact way but I
wasn't letting him off the hook because he came
with a few sweet words. I was tired of being
pushed around and picked back up by him.

I'm coming over
now.

> I'm not there
> so do whatever
> you want.

You left town
without telling
me?

> Yes, I left town
> without telling you.
> I don't answer to you
> anymore.

Vistoria, don't talk
like that. When will
you be back.

> I won't. I moved.
> For good.

Moved where?

> I'm in GA.

You thought it was

smart to move to
another city without
telling me?

That was kinda the
point Kich. I don't
want anything to do
with you. Get that
through your head.

Stupid Bitch.

Fuck you.

Fucking you, is
what everyone
has done. What
kind of woman
lets two brothers
fuck her? A hoe.

Oh there it goes.
You've wanted to
say that to me for
a while haven't you?
And let's be clear...
y'all aren't brothers.
Y'all are ugly ass
friends who grew
up on the same street.

And you're the
hoe we both
fucked. But I should

thank you. You did
a great job of sucking
and fucking us both
and treating us just
like the Kings we are.

                    You're crazy
                    and delusional.
                    And you're jealous
                    of Zay. Admit it?

Bitch, die. I
hope you wreck
the next time you
drive your car.

        My mouth dropped and I had to gasp for
air.
        *Did he just say that to me? What happened
to the Kich I thought I knew?*
        I wasn't going to let him know his
statement had gotten to me so deeply. Although by
now I was crying hard tears as I was punching
words into my phone.

                    I guess I hit a nerve.
                    I liked fucking him
                    more than you too.

That's fine.
At least I got
to get the pussy.
It was aight for
the time being.
You liked this dick

when it was in you
so that's all that
matters.

How was he still finding a way to be cocky
about his sex at a moment like this?

Whatever asshole.
You're blocked now.

I swam through all my social media
accounts blocking his name. I blocked his number
and blocked him anywhere I could think to block.
I stayed in my room for the rest of the night
crying. I felt like I was dying inside.
*Maybe this is karma for choosing them
both.*
I didn't understand why it all had to end so
badly when it seemed so good.
Seconds, minutes, hours, days, weeks, and
months passed. That's how I saw it. I saw and felt
every moment without one of them in my life. It
was like the absence of Kich made the absence of
Zay even thicker. With the time alone I could think
about what I really wanted. Honestly, I still loved
them both. But being in a different city at least
allowed me the luxury of not feeling pressured to
taking one of them back. Yes, Kich would've
followed me wherever I went, but he was crazy
and after he wished death upon me I didn't know if
it was safe to take him back.
*To Kich's defense I've heard my friends tell
their boyfriends to die plenty of times.*

It just hurt me differently because I had never said it and I never planned to tell another person to die.

After what I experienced with Kich and Zay I didn't know if I'd be able to go back to regular dating again. And I wasn't meeting anyone of interest since my new move.

One day after work I came home and took a relaxing shower. Once I was done I jumped in the bed and scrolled my Instagram. Nothing was really happening so I decided I should lurk. I hadn't lurked on Zay's or Kich's page in forever. Zay's page was now public so I could view it without using Kara's password. I got there and once again it was him and a group photo.

I hope they talk about bitches when they're together and have orgies because if I see one more group photo I'm going to assume they are fucking each other.

I laughed at myself then I read the caption.

zayphillips
Bro trip: ATL

Zay's in Atlanta? I bet that means Kich is here too.

I missed Zay, a lot. I was looking good and feeling good and I decided I wanted to see him. So I commented on one of his pictures.
storitime
Text me.

Now I wasn't expecting him to actually text me especially with everything that had gone on. But I actually had no proof whether or not Zay knew anything at all or if he hated me. I decided that this would be my way to see once and for all. If he's in town he's going to want to get freaky with someone and why not with some pussy you know was once yours. I mean there's no need in taking a chance with new pussy that might not give when you can get fo' sho pussy. At least that was my logic.

+1 (901) 000-7684

Sup.

Hi, stranger. What you doing in my city?

I had to find a quick way to let him know I was here. Zay is known for not texting me back.

Atlanta?

Yea, you didn't know I lived here now?

Naw, I didn't. What you doing today?

I'm headed to a Braves' game with some my friends.

Oh well we can meet up later then.

Ok cool, where are
you staying at?

The Hyatt.

Ok well I'll hit you
up later then.

Me and the girls went to see the Braves'
play. I always liked to get out and socialize in the
city. I was always that cliché person who had to
get a hotdog just because I was at a baseball game.
It just seemed like that was what you did. I loved
the food at the stadium. I ate my food and my
friend's food. It always worked out because they
loved desert and I didn't.

"I think I'm gonna go get ice cream," Kara
said.

"I want ice cream too," Cookie said.

"Well, I'll take the rest of your pizza," I
grabbed Kara's box.

"And your burger," I grabbed Cookie's
container.

I was like the leftover queen when it came
to eating out. It was my way of getting everything
I wanted without paying for it.

It was a good day. I talked to Zay a bit and
the Braves won the game. I was still wondering if I
was going to get to see him tonight or not. He had
stood me up the last time we were in Memphis so I
didn't know what to expect.

Zay

What are you doing?

Leaving this club?

Oh, did you have fun?

Yea it was straight.
How was the game?

Cool, we won.

Aww bet, that's
what's up.

So, did you still
want to meet up
or what?

I'm tryna see what
my dudes about to
do first.

Ok, let me know.

I was starting not to look forward to it
because Zay was acting funny with me before he
knew about Kich...there's no telling how he would
act now that he knows. Possibly... I still didn't
know if he knew for sure or not. I heard my phone
get an email so I went to check it.

Kich Mawni
Vistoria, I need you to forgive me. I'm so sorry.
Can I please see you? I'm in Atlanta. I need to see

you. I can't live without you.

I could see most of Kich's message before I opened it. I had to take a deep breath. I didn't know if I wanted to open it entirely to see what else he had written. I didn't want to be pulled back in by him. But part of me couldn't resist I had never seen Kich act this way.

Kich Mawni
I will not stop until you're back with me. I will do anything and go through anyone to have you.
Vistoria Jefferson
Kich none of that means anything to me. You don't know how to talk to me. You say really hurtful things to me and you think it's ok but it's not.
Kich Mawni
I know and I apologize. Vistoria I have wanted you since the 1st day I laid eyes on you. I never cared who you were with and I still don't. The meeting, that day you picked Zay up from my shoot, at the BBQ. I saw you and something went through me. I knew I would get you. I knew you were mine.

All of this felt so weird coming from Kich, but I didn't know if it was enough. What if it was just words to get me to act right while he was in town. I was hunting Zay while Kich was hunting me. It was a cycle it seemed that was never ending.
Vistoria Jefferson
Kich it's not enough.

Zay

Hey, our room
is packed so I'ma
just drive to you.

203

Didn't you say
you lived close?

Yea, I'm like
12 minutes
away.

That night all my energy shifted back. As I
gave myself to Zay I felt at home again. I felt like I
had the person I had fought for. The person I had
always wanted from the beginning. Kich was a
great guy but I would've never ended up with him
if Zay had just acted right in the 1st place. Did I
resent it? No. I loved every moment of it. I loved
every moment with Kich, but I don't think I loved
Kich enough. Kich shattered what love I had
growing for him as soon as it sprouted. Zay let my
love for him flourish.

These were all the thoughts going through
my head as we switched positions and Zay made
love to me. Zay was always passionate with all of
his movements. Deep, strong strokes that touched
my spine. Massages in between rounds. Slow
kisses down my back. It never failed Zay hit every
spot in me that needed some attention. Just like the
1st time he was the guy to get my drought. He had
perfect timing with that.

Once we finished we lied there in silence.
The moment with Zay was quiet and real. We
didn't speak for a long time. It was if we both had
silent apologies for something. I still didn't know if
he knew of my betrayal or not but if he did he
wasn't holding it against me.

Then a terror came up in me. What if Zay repeated his cycle and left again. Was I willing to keep putting my heart on the line for him? I started to feel something waking up in me. It was resentment. I started to feel a chill come over my body as I looked at him.

Reciprocity

I was hoping for love.
But all you were giving me was sex and attention.
On lonely nights it felt about equal.
I guess it wasn't right for me to ask you to wear a
shoe you never agreed to.
I didn't realize 'til now but that's what I really
wanted -love- but since I couldn't see it.
You were what I filled the void with.
Well I tried it, you just wouldn't fit.
My cup was always on empty.
There was no peace, only pressure of me trying to
convince myself that this was actually working.
I was searching for love but I settled for you.
You couldn't give what you didn't have.
I don't blame you for being who you were.
I blame me for acting like I couldn't see it.
You let me live. You were always right.
You let me learn. You always warned.
I gave it, myself to many.
I always felt empty.
Reciprocity?
Can someone show it?
They say men use love to get sex and women use
sex to get love.
With hidden motives already in play,
it seems lies is all we reciprocate.

Why should I choose? He's no better. He toys with my heart just like Kich. It's time for me to toy with some hearts. FUCK THAT! I'm tired.

You finally get it.

I rolled over once I realized Zay was asleep and I went back to my email.

Kich Mawni

Vistoria, let me make it up to you.

Vistoria Jefferson

Zay is here.

Kich Mawni

I don't give a fuck, come to me.

Vistoria Jefferson

Aren't all y'all together?

Kich Mawni

No, I'm staying longer so I got a different place. Send me your address I'm coming to pick you up.

Vistoria Jefferson

I can't just leave him here.

Kich Mawni

You're mine. I told you that. I don't give a damn. Send the address.

I emailed him my address and I figured at this point it was time for me to unblock him. Kich's hotel was up the road so it didn't take anytime for him to get there.

As I was exiting Cookie was in the kitchen pouring some wine.

"And where is your ass creeping out to? Looking like you 'bout to take out the trash," she joked.

"Taking out the trash" was a code often used by Cookie and her lovers when they needed to find a way to sneak off from their spouses or just a term when you were on some slick shit.

"I'm going to meet Kich," I said.

"Ain't Zay back there?" she said with a sharp look.

"Yes," I replied.

"My bitch," she gave me a high-five.

"It's about time you caught on. Play that shit like the game it is. You ain't married. You single, do what the fuck you want," she sipped from her wine.

"That's why I fucks with you," I said.

Cookie had a really big yard and a gate surrounding her entire house. I hit the code to open the gate as I was walking out to let Kich in. He parked and I ran up to him and kissed him.

He pushed me into his car and started fucking me right there on the hood.

"Don't you ever leave me again," he said.

"I won't," I moaned.

I loved the way my body sounded hitting against his car. He turned me over and started hitting it from the back as my hands were pressed against the car and one leg was raised up on the tire.

"You know no one can ever do you like I do you. I have so much to show you. I want to take you deeper into my world," he whispered in my ear.

I felt so free. I felt so alive. I felt like I was back in Kich's Power Room because I now felt it running through my veins. It was time for me to own myself and to do exactly what I wanted to do and when I wanted to do it. Restraints said I shouldn't see Kich because Zay was in the house. Restraints said I shouldn't fuck Kich because Zay had just fucked me. Well freedom said I could do whatever the hell I wanted and that's what I did.

Class is in session and it's "Stori Time" bitches!

THE END